A PINE CREEK WEDDING
THE COWBOYS OF PINE CREEK
BOOK FIVE

CHRISTINA BUTRUM

Copyright © 2023 by Christina Butrum

All rights reserved.

No part of this book may be reproduced in any form or by any electronic or mechanical means, including information storage and retrieval systems, without written permission from the author, except for the use of brief quotations in a book review.

Edited by: Three Owls Editing

Cover by: Daniel at thebookbrander.com

Formatted by: Christina Butrum

CHAPTER ONE

Andrea Martin's best friend was getting married, so of course, she happily accepted the role of not only being a bridesmaid but stepping in as the wedding planner as well. The invitation came as no surprise, really. Once she'd found out that Beckett had given Kate a second chance, she knew the rest would be history. Happily ever after and all.

Even though Andrea hadn't seen Kate since their last and final race together, the two of them spent hours on the phone each week, catching up and making plans for Kate's big day. At the time, when Kate first invited Andrea, the wedding date seemed to be lightyears away, but now, in less than two months, her best friend would be saying "*I do*."

Andrea was beyond thrilled for her best friend. She could only pray Kate's marriage lasted longer than hers had.

She dismissed the thought of needed prayers from her mind and focused on the highway in front of her. Just because her own marriage had ended unexpectedly short of happily ever after didn't mean every marriage was destined to end.

Besides, there was something to say about the love Beckett and Kate shared. Kate deserved the second chance Beckett had given her. Second chances were a sign of undeniable love. Not only that, but a love worth fighting for.

It was too bad there was no saving her own marriage. She would have fought tooth and nail if it hadn't been so obvious the two of them had grown apart. Sure, he could blame it on her love of racing and always being gone, but he had his fair share of faults, too. The only difference being that Andrea's didn't involve falling head over heels for another person and getting caught in the act.

Though it hurt, Andrea didn't allow herself to dwell on it. She filed for divorce, and thankfully, everything went smoother than she imagined it would have. Agreements were made and papers were signed without needing an attorney's help with the process. Again, Andrea thanked God for that answered prayer because even though she had several thousand dollars in the bank, half of which was split with her now ex-husband, she didn't have to sell her award-winning horse, Stella.

Andrea glanced in the rearview mirror, taking a second to check on the Logan Coach trailer attached to her truck. In hindsight, there was no way she could have sold Stella. Stella was everything to her. The two of them shared an incredible bond right from the start, but through the years of negative pregnancy tests and being told Andrea would never have children of her own, that bond had strengthened and the two of them became inseparable. Stella was worth much more to Andrea than the going rate of racehorses. Andrea's horse had become more like a best friend and an outlet for therapy when she needed it the most.

It seemed silly at the time, telling Stella things she'd rather not mention to others—including Kate, her best friend of several years. Heck, Kate still had no idea about Andrea's marriage falling apart. Even if given the chance, Andrea still wasn't sure if she would tell her.

Maybe when the time was right, but honestly, that

would most likely be never, or at least not until the wedding was officially done and the happy couple was back from their honeymoon. She knew Kate. There was no way Kate would continue making plans for her big day knowing her bestie was down and out. *And besides, what kind of wedding planner shares all the dreadful details of her failed marriage right before her best friend's wedding day?*

Andrea's thoughts were interrupted by an incoming call through her truck's Bluetooth. Kate's name scrolled across the screen, making it easy for Andrea to quickly accept the call.

"Hey, you," Andrea said, sounding chipper despite the thoughts running through her mind. "How's everything going?"

Kate blew out a ragged breath, sounding more exhausted than she normally would at this time of day. "I just got back from the dude ranch. I took it upon myself to get the cabin completely spotless and ready for your arrival."

Andrea felt a pang of guilt in her chest. "You didn't have to do that. I was willing to sleep on a stack of hay bales in the barn as long as I got to see you."

Muffling a laugh, Kate said, "I wouldn't have let you. Cleaning the cabins was long overdue. Our housekeeper quit last week, and it's the start of the busy season. Besides, it did me good to get out of the house and think of things other than my long list of to-dos."

"Well, okay, I guess." Andrea accepted Kate's reason and quickly added, "But you should be careful. You don't want to overdo it with a baby on the way."

Kate blew it off, much like Andrea expected her to, but she was being serious. Even though she hadn't experienced a pregnancy, and never would, Andrea knew what was recommended from months of her own research in between unsuccessful doctor visits.

"I can help when I get there," Andrea offered. Thanks to Kate, she was given the break she wanted —no, needed—from her life in Dallas. She was looking forward to seeing Kate and planning for the wedding. She would be lying if she said it didn't double as a distraction and time to think about what she was going to do next while staying in Pine Creek. "I'll have to earn my keep anyway, especially since Stella and I will be two more mouths to feed at the ranch."

Kate's laugh ricocheted through the speakers in the truck's cab. If Andrea didn't know any better, it sounded like her best friend was sitting right there beside her in the passenger seat. Instead, the passenger seat, along with the back, was full of Andrea's belongings. Or at least what she could grab and refused to leave behind.

"You know Porter and Diane are happy to have you," Kate said. "And Stella. I swear their motto around here has been "*the more the merrier*" since the good Lord knows when."

Andrea was comforted by the thought of Porter and Diane Carlson welcoming her with open arms. She imagined the two of them as replicas of her own parents—warm and inviting. If Andrea's parents were still alive, there was no doubt they would encourage her to just come home and start over with their help.

"Hunter and Alyssa have already made room for Stella," Kate explained, leaving Andrea feeling especially blessed for the ability to bring her horse along with her. "So, now we're just waiting for you two to get here."

Andrea didn't need to see her friend's face to know she was smiling. She could hear it. She tapped the screen and selected the navigational tool. "According to GPS, we'll be there in less than an hour."

Kate's excitement radiated through the speakers as she gave a short squeal. "I can't wait to see you."

"Same here. It feels like it's been forever." It was

weird how fast time went. It didn't seem possible that they hadn't seen each other in several months. Might as well have been forever.

"I hope you're hungry. Diane's got enough food here to feed an army," Kate said quickly. There was a ruckus in the background that Andrea could only imagine was a houseful surrounding Kate. The way Kate described the ranch, there was never a dull moment.

"And then some—" A man's voice cut in from somewhere beside Kate. Andrea assumed it might have been Beckett, but if not, at least one of the Carlson brothers she had yet to meet.

"Cut it out," an older woman hollered from the background. "It's my duty to make sure everyone gets plenty to eat around here. I wouldn't want anyone to go hungry."

"You heard her, Andie," Kate said, raising her voice over the others. "Plenty of food and love to go around."

Andrea smiled at the sentiment. From the start of her trip, she couldn't wait to get to Pine Creek, but now, she anticipated her arrival even more.

"See you in a few," Kate said, allowing the others in the background to say their goodbyes before ending the conversation.

Andrea clicked the button on her steering wheel, ending the call on her end, and smiled. Despite being broken recently, her heart did a happy dance in anticipation, expecting nothing but good things to come from this trip and her stay at Pine Creek Ranch.

CHAPTER TWO

Devon Carlson wanted to discuss a few things with his twin brother, Beckett. It wasn't until recently that talk of the wedding day became uncontrollable, and Devon was kind of tired of hearing about it. Every chance someone had to mention it, they did without hesitation. Luckily for him, he would never have to worry about planning, let alone participating in, his own wedding. He had yet to find a woman willing to accept him for who he was. He went to school with most of the available women in town, so he knew his chances of finding love were few and far between.

"We still have plenty of time, but Kate's already mentioned wanting hay bales for the guests at the wedding," Beckett informed him. "We're still waiting on RSVPs, but I don't think we'll need more than twenty or thirty."

Devon wasn't good at math, but he knew his brother was off in his calculations. "We have more than that in our family alone, not including friends from town."

Beckett scrubbed at his five o'clock shadow, seeming to think about it for a minute before he said, "You're probably right. Any chance you're willing to help me out with that?"

"With what? Herding people to your wedding?" Devon laughed. "That's all on you, bro. I'm just the best man. My job is to stand proudly at your side while you tie the knot and cut off your access to freedom."

That earned him a slug from Beckett. He rubbed his arm. "What was that for? I'm just stating the facts. What are you expecting me to do?"

The thought of preventing his brother from marrying Kate had never crossed his mind. The two of them were good together. But that didn't stop him from taking a few jabs at Beckett. It was all in good fun.

"Well, being my best man comes with a few requirements," Beckett said sternly. Unlike Devon,

Beckett took things a bit too seriously. Not that Devon really blamed him. If Beckett didn't take things like life on the ranch and settling down seriously, they would all think he was ill and needed to see a doctor.

"Like what?" Devon hadn't thought too much about accepting the role of best man. He would do anything for his twin brother. Or any of his brothers, in fact. But even then, there had to be a spot to draw the line. "I refuse to be matched up with a bridesmaid just to make for nice pictures, if that's what you're thinking."

Beckett shot him a look that told him he was out of his mind, but Devon knew better than to believe it was out of question. He knew his brothers. And not only that, but he also knew his mother. If she somehow got the slightest hint of attraction between Devon and a member of the wedding party, it would be game over.

"You act like that would be the end of the world," Beckett noted, shaking his head and adjusting his cowboy hat to block the mid-afternoon sun from his eyes.

"Might not be the end of the world, but I'm not willing to let anyone put reins on my freedom," Devon stated matter-of-factly, offering his brother a smug smile. "I'm not ready for all those honey-do lists that Kate leaves for you every morning."

Beckett got a kick out of that, regardless of the fact that Devon was as serious as a heart attack. He saw what being in love had done to his brothers, and there was no way he was getting involved in all that nonsense.

"It might do you some good," Beckett said with a snort. "It's about time you settle down and realize there's more to life than joking around and having fun."

Devon knew where his brother was coming from, but he didn't want anything to do with that. He took life on the ranch as seriously as the others, but when it came to love, he was drawing a line. A line he wasn't willing to cross anytime soon.

"I hate to say it, but you don't have much choice when it comes to the pictures."

Devon wanted to swipe that smirk off of his brother's face, but before he had a chance to act on it, their conversation was interrupted by none other than Kate Jacobsen, soon to be Carlson.

He held back a fake gag when Kate pecked his brother on the cheek. "Get a room. No one wants to see that."

Kate's lips parted to say something as Beckett slid

his hat off and blocked Devon's view from seeing more of their shared affection.

"Bleh." Devon cringed and shook his arms as though bugs were crawling on him. It was all in good fun, but it earned him a stern look from Beckett.

He could have left them to it, but he truly wanted to know what was expected from him in this wedding. He could wait until the two of them were done smooching and giving each other puppy dog eyes—he would just look the other way.

Thankfully, Kate broke the spell she had on his brother and stepped back. "I just wanted to let you guys know that Andie will be here any minute now."

Devon raised a brow and shot Beckett a look but remained quiet.

"Andrea," Beckett clarified. "Kate invited her to the ranch in order to get things ready."

Devon already knew that. He'd overheard Kate telling the others outside. He'd also confronted Kate with his opinion about getting the ranch ready for the wedding. In his mind, all that was needed was to set up tables and chairs and call it a done deal.

"I still don't see why it's going to take two months." Devon wasn't trying to be smart. It was an honest-to-God question. "Who needs two months to prepare for a wedding?"

Unlike Beckett, Kate didn't mind his questions. Kate was laid-back and down-to-earth, fitting in with the rest of them at the ranch, but she had one up on Beckett when it came to rolling with the punches and having fun. There was no doubt in Devon's mind Kate would never be called a *Bridezilla*.

Kate's smile dropped into a slight frown, though, and Devon couldn't help but wonder if he might've struck a nerve. Maybe his sarcasm and jokes had gone too far.

"She's been going through a lot ever since she quit racing," Kate explained, keeping her tone light and pleasant. "I thought it would do her some good to get away and take her mind off of things for a while."

Devon glanced at Beckett, searching for recognition in his brother's eyes. Of course, his brother nodded knowingly, so Devon decided to accept it for what it was.

"Okay, my bad," he said. Then, he quickly mumbled, "Sorry."

"It's okay," Kate said with a shrug. "I mainly just wanted to give you a heads up that she's almost here. She'll be staying in one of our spare cabins. Porter and Diane already know, and they're looking forward to meeting her."

Devon nodded, never knowing a time when his

parents weren't anticipating someone's arrival at the ranch.

"I'm excited to have her help with the wedding," Kate said with a smile. "We've been talking about things for months. It's going to be a lot of fun."

As though Beckett sensed a dumb remark forming in Devon's mind, he shot him a look that warned him to keep quiet. Devon zipped his lips and agreed to do whatever Kate needed from him. He wouldn't mention drawing the line. That would stay between the brothers.

Kate pecked Beckett on the cheek one last time before heading back to the main house. She turned back and called out to Devon, "I don't think you'll have anything to worry about. I think everyone's going to love her."

"Everyone but me," Devon mumbled under his breath, earning him another slug in the arm. "Cut it out. You didn't need to do that."

"That's the least of your worries if you don't act right while she's here," Beckett warned, narrowing his eyes at Devon. "You better be on your best behavior."

"Okay, Dad," Devon retorted, ducking away in time to dodge another slug on the arm.

"I mean it." Beckett was the same age as Devon,

being his twin and all, but he was acting way older than twenty-five.

"Have a little fun in your life, Beck," Devon said, resisting the urge to rub his arm.

"This isn't going to be some wild party, Dev. It's my wedding," Beckett stated firmly. "You can have fun, but like everything else, there's a limit."

"You act like I'm going to shove the poor woman in a pile of manure and laugh about it." Devon would never do such a thing, for one, and for two, he wasn't a jerk. No matter what, he was a gentleman, and he always would be. "Have a little more faith in me than that, would you?"

Beckett seemed to agree to disagree with a curt nod. It wouldn't be long before the two of them wrapped up their morning chores and headed to the main house for lunch.

Devon was looking forward to eating lunch with the family, but he could say with certainty that he wasn't looking forward to meeting whoever would be joining them. He had a bad feeling about it, and if there was any truth in the last thing Kate had said, he needed to be prepared not to love, or even *like*, Andrea.

CHAPTER THREE

Everything Kate said about the ranch and what to expect was spot-on—right down to the littlest details, including the color of the horse barn where Hunter and Alyssa trained horses to the wraparound front porch and little wooden swing on the main house.

The sight of the ranch made Andrea's heart dance happily inside her chest. She knew from the conversations she'd had with Kate that the Carlsons' property was to die for, but she didn't quite expect it to be this extravagant. The property ran for miles, spreading across acres of land surrounded by pine trees and cabins on the north side and cattle grazing mindlessly in pastures to the east and west. This was every cowgirl's dream come true.

It made perfect sense why Kate decided to stay. If given the opportunity, Andrea wouldn't bat an eye. It beat the small, ranch-style home she had resided in for the last couple of years.

Andrea spotted Kate standing in the distance by the paddock as she turned off the highway and into the entrance where a *Welcome to Pine Creek Ranch* sign hung nearby. If she had to guess, Kate had been counting down the minutes until Andrea's arrival—timing it down to the minute to be the first to welcome her to the ranch.

Andrea steered the truck into a vacant spot next to the barn, making sure to leave enough room for the trailer before shifting into park. She couldn't wait to get out and wrap her arms around her best friend.

No sooner had her boots touched the ground than she wrapped Kate in a bear hug, refusing to let go until they were both standing there in tears.

"It's been so long," Kate said, squeezing Andrea. "I've missed you so much."

"I've missed you more." Andrea bit her quivering lip, a failed attempt to hide the emotional tremble in her voice. "You have no idea how much I've missed you."

Andrea dropped her arms at her side and took a step back. She looked Kate up and down, then grinned. Kate modeled the baby bump just how Andrea imagined she would—wearing cute short overalls, cowgirl boots, and a pink mama-to-be shirt. Cue the waterworks for the second time. "You look wonderful!"

Kate's face lit up as tears sparkled in her eyes. She swiped a finger underneath her eye and said, "Thank you. You look great yourself. I still can't believe you're here."

"You must be Andrea?" A cowboy walked up beside them and offered Andrea his hand. "I'm Hunter. I'm in charge of taking care of the horses and getting them trained around here. Would you like me to unload your horse and get her in the barn so the two of you have time to catch up?"

Andrea shared a quick look with Kate and said, "Yes, that would be great. Thank you."

She watched as Hunter made his way to the back of the trailer and unlatched the door. "Are they all that good-looking and charming?"

Kate stifled a laugh but nodded. "Yes, the Carlson brothers are one of a kind. True gentlemen. Just wait until you meet them all."

"Six, right?"

"That's right," Kate said, turning her attention back to Andrea. "A few might seem a little rough around the edges, but deep down they've got the biggest hearts."

They stood off to the side of the barn, watching as Hunter led Stella out of the trailer and into the barn. The way he moved with the horse, there was no doubt he knew how to handle her.

"Well, who do we have here?" An older man peeked around the edge of the trailer and smiled. He walked up and extended his hand just as Hunter had. "You must be Andie. Kate's told us a lot about you."

Andrea looked at Kate and said, "Hopefully all good things, right?"

The older man's laugh rumbled in his throat as he released Andrea's hand. "All good things for sure." After a short pause, he said, "I'm Porter, by the way. You can just call me 'Port,' or perhaps 'Pops' like the rest of them do around here. Just don't call me 'sir' or 'late to dinner.'"

He patted her on the arm and shot her a wink. "It's good to have you here. I'm sure you're going to have your hands full, but don't be afraid to ask for whatever you might need."

"Will do. Thank you," Andrea confirmed as Porter tipped his hat and headed for the barn.

She turned back to Kate and asked, "There's no

doubt who they got their good looks and manners from, is there?"

"No, but I'm sure Diane has a say in that." Kate hooked a thumb over her shoulder. "Let's head to the main house so you can meet her. She's been impatiently waiting for you to get here."

Andrea agreed to walk with Kate, allowing her to lead as she waved at everyone they met along the way. Kate stopped at the bottom of the porch and turned to face Andrea. A look of concern crossed her face, and for a minute, Andrea's heart skipped a beat and her stomach dropped. "What's wrong?"

She knew her friend wasn't more than six months along, because her due date was a month, give or take, after the wedding, but what if?

"Kate, are you okay?"

Her friend's face flushed, and she didn't look well. Andrea's heart sped up, beating into overdrive against her ribs. She wrapped her arms around Kate, guiding her to sit on the porch step. Andrea straightened, keeping her hand on Kate's shoulder for fear of her falling forward, as she looked around for someone to help.

"Hey!" She called out to a man walking out of a long shed nearby. He was across the driveway, but certainly he had to hear her, right? "Hey!" she shouted a little louder this time, praying he would hear her shout for help and would come running.

Thankfully, he did hear her. A look of panic crossed his face as he raced toward them. "What happened? Kate, are you alright?"

Kate mumbled something under her breath. Andrea was trained in first aid and CPR, but she wasn't sure she knew how to handle this.

"Someone needs to get Beck," the cowboy told Andrea, but she didn't know who Beckett was. She'd talked about him with Kate and had seen him once—but that was several months ago when he came to watch Kate's last race. When the man realized Andrea wasn't moving, he jumped to his feet and said, "Stay with her. I'm going to grab Beckett and call for an ambulance."

"Kate, talk to me," Andrea begged, pleading with her friend to say something. She checked for signs of bleeding or anything that would alert to—*No, it can't be that.* Andrea shook the thought away and knelt before Kate on the bottom step. "Kate, look at me."

Only when Kate lifted her chin and looked Andrea in the eyes, she could tell something really wasn't right with her. She looked weak, too weak to speak, and there were a million things running through Andrea's mind as to what could be wrong.

"Kate, babe." A man wearing a black cowboy hat ran up to the steps and knelt beside Andrea. He reached out and took Kate's hand, giving it a gentle squeeze. "The ambulance is on the way. Are you in pain? What happened?"

A look of panic crossed his face as he glanced over to Andrea. He searched for answers, but Andrea wasn't much help. "She was just fine a moment or two ago. We were talking and laughing… We were getting ready to head inside."

The man she now assumed to be Beckett raised a hand and placed it on Kate's forehead. "Did she say anything? Complain of any pain?"

"I'm fine," Kate mumbled in a hushed whisper. "I just need to go inside and cool down."

Beckett glanced over his shoulder as the sound of footsteps crunched on the gravel behind them. Another man, roughly the same age as Beckett, approached them and asked, "What's going on? Is she okay? It's not the baby, is it?"

Andrea tried to remain calm. It was the best she could do when her friend needed assistance, but this man's questions weren't helping. No one had the answers to his questions. Andrea prayed it wasn't the baby. From everything she read and learned in the past few years, it didn't look like this was pregnancy related. She prayed she was right.

The sound of sirens echoed in the distance as an ambulance barreled down the highway toward the ranch. It slowed as it turned off the highway and onto the driveway leading them to where everyone stood around Kate.

Andrea took a step back when two EMTs wheeled a stretcher to the gathering area. They were asking questions much like Beckett and the other two had. Questions she didn't have the answers to.

Beckett helped lift Kate from the porch step, filling the EMTs in on how far along she was, most recent meal, medications, and any known allergies. Beckett spit the information out faster than Andrea expected him to, which made her grateful Kate had a man like Beckett.

Watching everything unfold caused her to question whether her ex-husband would have been able to rattle off her medications and allergies, let alone the last meal she ate.

"She'll be okay," said the man who had rushed to their side. He adjusted his hat and stood close to Andrea. "I'm sure she's just been overdoing it lately. Beckett's told her to take it easy more than once. And with the summer heat…"

His words trailed off, and Andrea could only pray it was exhaustion or the heat, and nothing to do with the baby. She didn't want her best friend to experience the same kind of loss she experienced a short time ago.

"Would you like to ride along with me?" His question interrupted Andrea's painful memory. She tore her eyes away from the highway and focused on what he was asking her. "We can meet them at the hospital, if you'd like?"

"Sure, um." She paused, looking around the property. Everyone was gathered around the main house, watching in shock and wondering if Kate was going to be okay. Porter wrapped his arm around a woman's shoulders, and Andrea assumed her to be Diane—the woman the two of them were on their way to see. The woman Kate so badly wanted Andrea to meet.

"Or you can wait here with Ma," the man said. "I'm sure she wouldn't mind the company."

Andrea looked back at Porter and Diane, knowing the woman wouldn't mind, but she needed to be with her friend. She needed to make sure she was okay.

"I'll go," Andrea said, and she followed the man to a white, rusted-out truck parked near what she assumed to be a cattle barn.

"Let me get the door for you," he said, rushing to

the passenger side of the truck. "It sometimes sticks, and you have to be a little rough with it to get it to open."

With an aggressive yank, the door opened, and the man patiently waited for Andrea to climb in, warning her to watch out for the splinter of rust hanging on the edge of the running board.

Before Andrea had a chance to question whether the truck would make it to the hospital, they were pulling out of the driveway and onto the highway.

"You must be Andrea," the man said, sliding his hat back and glancing over at her. "I'm Devon, by the way."

Even though her mind was racing and she was worried about Kate, she welcomed the small talk as a much-needed distraction. And it didn't hurt that he assured her in the most comforting tone that Kate would be alright.

CHAPTER FOUR

Devon didn't mind Andrea coming along with him to the hospital. He would be lying if he said he wasn't trying to earn bonus points, though. Maybe if he got to know her before all of the wedding planning went into effect, Andrea would take it easier on him when it came to bossing him around—even though Kate promised her best friend wouldn't be like that.

"Kate's said a lot about you," Devon said, not sure what to say to break through the awkward silence in the cab of his truck. "You're a barrel racer, right?"

"Not anymore," Andrea said quietly.

He didn't have the heart to tell her to speak up. He could barely hear her over the rumble of his truck's exhaust. She was looking out the window, appearing a little uncomfortable given the situation.

He could have just left it at that, ending the attempt to talk on their way to the hospital, but now he was curious as to why she didn't race anymore. He knew why Kate no longer raced, but he had a feeling the reason wasn't the same for Andrea.

Thankfully, he didn't have to ask the reason why she gave it up. She looked over at him, repositioning herself in the passenger seat, possibly an attempt at getting more comfortable. His truck was older than dirt, but aside from the lack of cushion in the seats and a little rust, it was reliable.

"Stella was ready to retire," she said with a shrug. "And things weren't going so great anyway."

Devon heard the emotion in Andrea's voice. He wouldn't press her for more on the subject. Instead, he changed the direction of their conversation.

"So," he said, wrapping his fingers around the steering wheel and looking straight ahead. "You'll be at the ranch until after the wedding?"

It was a dumb question. He already knew the answer, but he didn't like the pained expression that crossed Andrea's face when she talked about not racing anymore.

"Yeah. Kate invited me to stay. She said no one would mind if I came a little earlier than planned."

Was she questioning if he minded whether she stayed at the ranch or not? He couldn't really tell, but judging by the raise of her brow, she might need some reassurance that Kate was correct in her assumption.

"Yeah, I don't think anyone really cares that you'll be staying at the ranch." He could have slapped himself for the way that came out. He didn't mean it like no one *cared* she was there. "I mean... I don't think anyone minds the extra company. They're glad to have you there."

A half-hearted smile pulled at Andrea's lips, as though she believed he was just saying that. As if that was how he felt as well. He might as well get it out of the way.

"I already told Kate that I'd help wherever I'm needed," he said, shrugging a shoulder. "Even though I don't think it's going to take all that much to set up for the wedding. Just a few tables and chairs, and call it good."

Andrea raised a brow but remained quiet as she studied him. *Uh oh, that can't be good.* He must have said something she disagreed with. It was too soon to get on her bad side.

He quickly corrected himself, hoping to play it off

without causing a rift between them. "But like I said, I'm willing to do whatever's needed. Just say what needs fixed, and I'll fix it."

That seemed to placate the rift for now if the questioning look Andrea was giving him was any indication.

"What?"

"Oh, nothing." She flashed an innocent smile. "Kate mentioned something about you being Mr. Fix It on the ranch."

Well, Kate wasn't wrong. He'd earned that title, and he was proud of it. He could fix anything. Well almost anything. If it could be fixed, he'd fix it.

"I really hope she's okay," Andrea said. There was that look of uncertainty in her eyes again, and Devon didn't know how to comfort her in a way she'd believe him.

"We're almost there," he said, taking his eyes off the road and glancing over at her. "It's just up ahead, about a mile or so."

Andrea nodded but stayed silent, which was okay with Devon. He wasn't much for talking anyway. The only thing on his mind at the moment was getting to the hospital and being there for his brother and soon-to-be sister-in-law. He silently prayed Kate and the baby would be fine and they were back at the ranch before too long.

Devon pulled the truck into the parking lot designated for the emergency room, found a vacant spot near the entrance, and shifted into park. He glanced over at Andrea and offered a half-smile before climbing out of the driver's seat.

He hurried to the passenger side and held the door as Andrea stepped out. He gave the door a forceful shove, making sure it latched properly before turning his attention back to Andrea. The last time he was at the emergency room had been a while back. He was fixing the gate on one of their pastures when their bull charged him unexpectedly and pinned him. Thankfully, he'd walked away with just a few bruised ribs and a lesson learned. It could have been a lot worse, especially if Beckett hadn't been standing by when it happened.

He shook the thought from his mind and opened the door for Andrea once they reached the entrance. He followed Andrea through the lobby until they reached the receptionist's desk. The receptionist smiled up at them as they approached the desk.

"Can I help you?"

Devon swiped his hat off and clutched it at his

side. "We're here to see Kate Jacobsen. She was brought in by ambulance a few minutes ago."

The receptionist studied the computer screen in front of her and nodded with a smile. "Yes, Kate's currently being seen in the ER, but you can have a seat in the waiting room if you'd like. I'll let the staff know you're here."

Devon wanted to argue with the younger woman working behind the counter, but instead, he agreed to leave it at that. The staff would let Beckett know they were there, and it would only be a matter of time before he came out with an update.

Andrea paused near the counter, hesitating a moment before following him. It seemed she might want to argue with the woman as well, but she decided against it. There was no need to make a scene. It wouldn't do anyone any good.

He led Andrea to the waiting room—the same waiting room his family had gathered in throughout the years. There was never a dull moment on the ranch, and sometimes that meant getting setback by a visit to the emergency room.

Andrea sat down beside him, a worried look on her face. He wasn't good at finding the right words to say in times like this, but he at least had to try.

"I'm sure everything's going to be alright," Devon assured her, though he wasn't convinced by his own words. What if something happened to the baby? What if something happened to Kate? He hated to think what that would mean for Beckett—for his family. He shifted in his chair. There was no reason to expect the worst. "Kate's a tough one. This isn't her first time in the ER."

Andrea's eyes widened in surprise at that. *Does she not know about the tumble Kate had from her horse when she first arrived at the ranch?* he wondered. Was it Devon's place to tell her? *Surely Kate had told her best friend, right?*

"Hey," Beckett called out as he entered the waiting area, saving Devon from saying something he possibly shouldn't. Devon and Andrea both stood and met Beckett halfway into the room. Beckett ran a hand through his matted hair and let out a relieved breath. "She's fine. The baby's fine. They have her hooked up to all kinds of machines, and they're giving her fluids."

Devon exchanged a glance with Andrea, who seemed to be just as relieved to hear Kate and the baby were okay.

"What happened? Do they know?" Andrea's voice trembled as she stood beside Devon. Maybe she wasn't as relieved at the news as Devon had thought. "Can I see her?"

Beckett took a step to the side and offered what information he could. "The doctor seems to think she's just dehydrated, but they're running tests to be sure. They're getting in touch with our family doctor as we speak."

Devon reached out and placed a hand on Beckett's shoulder. "I'm sure everything's fine. Being dehydrated is no joke, and it makes sense. Kate's hardly known for taking it easy and resting when she should."

He shared a light chuckle with his brother, but Andrea didn't seem too impressed with what he said. If she had something on her mind, she wasn't willing to share it judging by the way she looked at him. So much for making nice.

Devon shrugged. *Oh well, it isn't about Andrea anyway.* Maybe he'd been right in assuming she was just another barrel racing diva. Time would eventually tell, and maybe then he could tell Beckett that he told him so.

But for now, the focus was on Kate and whether she was coming home soon. Devon wouldn't leave his brother without a ride back to the ranch, and he was certain Beckett wouldn't leave without Kate by his side.

"If you want, you two can head back to the ranch," Beckett offered, running another hand through his hair. "I'd hate to keep you guys waiting. It could be a few hours until she's released and ready to head home."

Unless they keep her overnight for observation. Devon kept that to himself. He didn't need to add unnecessary worry to the situation.

"Are you sure?" Devon exchanged a look with Andrea, who appeared to disagree with the idea of leaving the hospital. She could stay as long as she wanted, but Devon would take his brother's word and head back to the ranch… if that's what Beckett wanted.

"Yeah," Beckett said, releasing a heavy sigh. "We'll be fine here. I'll call if anything changes."

Devon gave his brother a quick squeeze on his shoulder. "We'll be waiting. Is there anything you need me to do back home?"

Beckett shook his head. Devon knew there was a list of things to mark off on Beckett's plate, but of course, his brother wasn't going to pass it off to anyone. They were all the same, really. Never wanting to burden anyone with a task they could handle themselves.

Devon would check in with Adam once they arrived home. Adam would tell him what needed to be done, and Devon would get to work without being told twice.

Even though Andrea didn't seem pleased about leaving the hospital, she followed Devon out of the waiting area and down the hall toward the exit. She hadn't spoken more than a few words since finding out Kate's condition wasn't life-threatening, but she seemed comforted knowing both Kate and the baby would be okay.

Devon yanked on the passenger door and held it open as Andrea climbed into the cab of his truck. He rounded the front of the truck and hopped into the driver's seat. Once the old truck fired up, he shifted into drive and headed for the highway.

"Have you met Ma and Pops yet?" he asked, breaking the silence between them.

"Not your mom," Andrea said, fidgeting with the hem of her shirt. "Kate was getting ready to introduce us when…"

Her words trailed off, and that's when Devon did the unthinkable. He reached out and placed his hand on her arm, wanting to assure her that everything was okay. He jerked it back, realizing he needed to keep his hands to himself and trying to ignore the fact it sent a jolt through him like he'd touched an electric fence.

Maybe that was a sign to keep his distance, or maybe it meant something else entirely. Either way, he would play it safe. He didn't need to tempt fate, and he certainly didn't need to give anyone the wrong impression.

CHAPTER FIVE

Back at the ranch, Andrea found her footing without the help from her best friend. With direction from Devon, she made her way to the main house and knocked on the door, knowing she would be more than welcomed by his parents.

She glanced over her shoulder as she waited for someone to come to the door. Devon was nowhere in sight. The moment he parked the truck and they climbed out, he pointed her toward the house and beelined it for the calving barn. He was on a mission to find his brother and get back to work.

"What on heaven's earth are you standing out here for?" A woman's voice startled Andrea, pulling her focus away from the barn. "Like I tell everyone else around here… there's no sense in knocking. Just come right in."

Andrea stepped inside, immediately taken back to her younger days when she would visit her grandparents. They'd owned a house much like this one, almost identical in fact—right down to the rooster décor in the kitchen.

"Come on in and have a seat," the woman, Andrea assumed to be Diane, said before pulling out a chair at the table and patting the cushion with a heartfelt smile. "I just heard the news from Beckett. He called not too long ago. Right before you and Devon returned. Kate's going to be okay. Doctor says she's dehydrated and will need to take it easy for a while, but she and the baby are going to be just fine."

Even though Andrea had heard the news firsthand from Beckett while standing in the waiting room, hearing it once more assured her that everything was going to be okay. Tears pricked her eyes at the thought of something terrible happening to Kate. They hadn't been friends for all that long, but they'd grown close through their years of barrel racing.

"I'm Diane, by the way, but everyone around here just calls me 'Ma.' You're welcome to call me whatever you'd like." Diane placed a glass of iced tea in front of Andrea and smiled. "I'm happy you're here to help Kate out with all of the wedding preparations. Lord knows that me and her mama are getting up there in age, and neither one of us can decorate like we used to."

Before Andrea could mention there were no worries and that she was more than willing to handle everything that needed to be taken care of, Diane continued, "But that's not to say we're not looking forward to the dress shopping and all that fun stuff. We've been waiting our entire lives for those two to tie the knot."

Andrea shared a laugh with Diane, realizing the woman shared quite a few similarities with her mother. No sooner had the memory of telling her mother the news about her own wedding came to mind than Andrea shook it away.

"I don't know how Kate's going to take the news from the doctor," Diane said, interrupting Andrea's thoughts. Andrea brought the cold drink to her lips and took a sip, nodding along and agreeing with Diane. She knew Kate better than anyone, and she knew Kate didn't like sitting around and *taking it easy*. There was a chance that phrase wasn't even in Kate's vocabulary. That woman never took it easy and was always ready for the next challenge life threw at her.

"I suppose she won't take it too well," Andrea said, setting the glass down in front of her. "But I'll make sure she knows I'm here for whatever she needs."

Diane smiled and patted Andrea's arm, seeming pleased to hear it. The screen door cracked against the wooden frame as the sound of heavy footsteps rounded the corner of the dining room from the kitchen. Porter approached the table and pulled out a chair. He sat down, reaching for the newspaper and glancing over at Andrea. "Quite the commotion around here, huh? If there's one thing to know, there's never a dull moment. But I'm glad to hear Kate and the baby are going to be alright. She's not going to like being laid up in bed all day, though."

Andrea exchanged a look with Diane, the shock factor registering in each of their expressions.

"Are you saying Kate's on bed rest?" Diane questioned Porter anxiously while Andrea held onto what little hope she had that things would go back to normal for Kate once she arrived back home from the hospital. "I don't think she'll like that at all. She goes stir-crazy when it rains and she can't get out of the house to do anything. Can you imagine what she's going to do now that she can't?"

"I can, and that's what I'm afraid of." Porter

unfolded the newspaper and glanced over the pages while wearing a pair of readers. Andrea sat quietly, listening to the interaction between the two carrying on about Kate. Porter took off his glasses and placed them beside him on the table before clasping his hands in front of him. "Speaking of which, did you know the housekeeper quit? Apparently, I'm the last to know about it. Lacy and Mya have been helping Kate out with the cabins at the dude ranch but failed to tell me. Which might explain why Kate's in the position she's currently in. She's taking on too much, and I have a feeling she knew I wouldn't be too happy about it. The same for the others, too. Everyone's spread thin around here, but there's no sense in not telling me anything."

"I know, Port," Diane said, reaching out and placing a hand on top of his. "I'm sure they just don't want to get you worked up and worried over something they can take care of, is all."

Porter's brow furrowed, seeming to contemplate if what Diane said was true or not. He shook his head, deciding to disagree. "And now look where they're at. Kate landed herself at the hospital, and thankfully she's okay, but now we're down for cleaning the cabins and guiding the trail riders. Lacy and Mya have their own things to do, and that's true for all of us."

"I can help," Andrea piped in, interrupting Porter's rant and causing both him and Diane to turn their attention to her. She offered a soft smile, feeling a little less confident than she had a moment ago, but still ready to jump in and get started wherever she might be needed. "I don't mind at all. Just tell me what you need done, and I'll do it."

She was there to help Kate, but honestly, what kind of friend would she be if she didn't offer? The Carlson family seemed nice enough, willing to let her stay at the ranch until the wedding. It was the least she could do while she was there, right?

CHAPTER SIX

Devon was mending yet another hole in the fence line when he caught sight of Andrea leaving the main house with his father by her side. He was a few hundred feet from the house, positioned just to the right of the bull pen, but he still had a clear view from where he sat.

He went back to work on the fence, minding his own business until the sound of gravel crunching under footsteps neared him. A quick glance over his shoulder confirmed what he imagined was going to happen.

"How's everything going out here, son?" his father called out, approaching him with Andrea in tow. "Ruby's bringing Beckett and Kate back home soon, and I know Kate won't be up to showing Andrea around the ranch."

Devon appreciated his father's concern for Kate, but he didn't appreciate where his father's thought process was going. He could only imagine what his father told Andrea while visiting in the house. He didn't have time to give Andrea a tour of the place, but he knew better than to argue with his father.

"So, you want me to be the one to show her around?"

One look at Andrea, and he knew he shouldn't have said it like that. He hadn't meant for his question to come out so harshly. He meant to keep his tone light and friendly. So much for that. She probably thought he was a jerk and doubted everything he said about how willing he was to step in and lend a hand where needed. Not that his offer had anything to do with showing her around.

"Well, if you don't mind," his father said, giving Devon a look that told him he was out of line. "She'll need to get settled into her cabin, too. I'm sure Owen wouldn't mind taking a break if you—"

"I can." Devon hated the thought of Owen showing Andrea around. Not that his brother couldn't handle the task, it was just... he knew his brother didn't care much about hospitality. He hadn't earned the title of "*Grinch*" for nothing—and it wasn't just around Christmastime.

"Good to hear." His father slapped a hand on his shoulder and gave it a firm squeeze. "The fence can wait until later anyway. Adam won't be bringing the cattle back to this pasture until morning."

Devon understood the assignment. His father wasn't giving him an option. With that, he looked at Andrea and said, "Let me get cleaned up a bit, and I'll meet you back here."

She glanced over at the barn and back to him. "I'll go check on Stella while you do that. I'm sure she's been waiting to see me."

Devon smiled, appreciating the fact that she cared about her horse. It said a lot about a person when they put animals first. "Alright, then. I'll meet you at the barn and help you unhook the trailer before it gets too late."

"Thank you."

His father clapped his hands and said, "Well, looks like my work here's done. I'm going to head inside and see if your mother needs help with anything before I take my usual nap before supper."

Devon held back a laugh as his father headed back to the main house. He didn't have a chance to say anything about his father's daily routine to Andrea, because she was well on her way to the barn to check on her horse.

He grunted, pulling off his gloves and shoving them into his back pocket. If he was lucky, he could show Andrea around, get her settled into her cabin, and have the fence fixed before suppertime.

First, he needed to wash up. Deciding the main house was closer, he headed in that direction, noting the time on his watch. Time was on his side. It wasn't as late as he expected it to be. That was good. Everything would go according to plan and leave him plenty of time to check in with Beckett and Kate once they got back home.

"What do you think of Andrea?"

His mother's question tore his attention from scrubbing his hands clean in the bathroom sink. She leaned on the doorjamb, watching him and patiently waiting for him to answer.

He shrugged as he reached for the hand towel. "She seems nice."

His mother shot him a grin, and he couldn't help but wonder what she was thinking. He could only imagine. He lost count of the conversations he'd had with her about finding a good woman, settling down, and making plans for the future. It certainly didn't help matters when all his brothers except Owen had found *the one*, and now she was expecting the same for the rest of them. But he was in no rush to settle down—especially not with someone like Andrea. Once a barrel racing diva, always a diva. Or so it seemed anyway.

"Well, I'll let you be," his mother said, backing out of the doorway. "Your father said you're going to show her around the ranch. I think that's awfully nice of you for offering since Kate won't be able to."

Devon furrowed his brow but quickly relaxed. He didn't have time to set the record straight. He'd let his mother believe whatever she wanted to believe.

"Make sure you invite her to supper," his mother called after him, getting in the last word as he walked out the door and onto the porch, the door closing behind him.

He grinned at his mother's antics. Of course, she wanted to play it off as him inviting Andrea to supper with the family. He was used to her mischief when it came to these kinds of things. He would make sure Andrea knew his mother wanted her to join them for supper. He was staying out of it.

"Hey," he called out as he entered the barn. He found Andrea exactly where she said she would be—standing in front of the stall and spending time with her horse. He walked down the aisle and stopped, leaving enough distance between them. "Are you ready?"

He didn't want to rush her, but time was ticking. The sooner he could show her the ranch and to her cabin, the sooner he could complete his tasks in time for supper.

"Yeah," Andrea said, running a hand through the horse's mane. "I was just promising Stella that I'd take her riding tomorrow. She's used to getting her daily exercise."

"It does them good," Devon stated, thinking about his own horse and how their time together wasn't much like it used to be.

"Porter mentioned a group will be here tomorrow for trail rides," Andrea said, still offering her horse attention. "I figured it'd be the perfect time to get Stella out for some fresh air. She enjoys slow walks every now and then, don't you, girl?"

Devon watched the exchange between Andrea and Stella. The horse nudged Andrea's hand, almost as if she acknowledged what Andrea said was correct. He shared a quick laugh with Andrea before glancing at his watch.

Andrea must have noticed, because no sooner had he checked the time than she said goodbye to Stella and followed him out of the barn toward her truck still attached to the Logan Coach trailer.

He wondered what she thought about his truck compared to hers. It was obvious her truck was brand new, not to mention the trailer. He could imagine the kind of money she had to acquire such a fancy setup like that.

But none of that mattered. It didn't matter what she thought about his truck. It didn't matter what kind of money she had. He wouldn't let himself get caught up in a situation like that again. He'd been there, done that. After his ex-girlfriend proved he wasn't good enough for a lavish lifestyle, he would just as soon stay single for the rest of his life. He was happy living the simple life anyway.

CHAPTER SEVEN

Andrea pulled the truck ahead on Devon's cue and heard the familiar sound of the latch unhooking from the back of her truck. She shifted into park and climbed out, meeting Devon at the tailgate.

"Thank you for helping me with this," she said, knowing he was going out of his way to help her. She'd seen the look he gave Porter when his father mentioned getting her settled in. She could only hope she wasn't wasting too much of his time. "I know you have plenty of other things you'd rather be doing."

He straightened from the hitch after unlatching the cables and looked at her. His brown eyes filled with something she couldn't quite read before he said, "It's fine. I don't mind at all."

She left it at that, hoping he was telling the truth. She was at the ranch to help with the wedding. The last thing she wanted was to become a thorn in someone's side.

After a moment of awkward silence, Devon walked to the side of the truck and opened the door for her. "Go ahead and hop in. You drive. I'll guide you."

With a smile, she did as Devon asked and climbed into the driver's seat of her truck. Her heart skipped a few beats at the thought of driving through unfamiliar grounds, but she calmed her nerves once Devon shut her door and made his way over to the passenger side. He climbed into the cab of her truck and buckled in, removing his hat once it hit the roof.

She stifled a quiet laugh, realizing he was much taller than she thought. Taking a deep breath, ready for the adventure ahead, she released it slowly and shifted into drive. "Where am I heading?"

"That way," Devon said, pointing her in the direction he wanted her to go. Her heart beat wildly in her chest, though she wasn't sure what the big deal was. She needed to relax. "Up ahead, right before we reach the trees, there'll be a fork in the road. You'll want to take a left."

She nodded, slowly pressing her foot down on the

accelerator and focusing on the gravel drive ahead of them. She wondered where they would end up if she took a right instead of a left, but instead of asking Devon, she decided she would find out soon enough.

The trees lined the north side of the property, providing a glimpse at the image Kate had illustrated in Andrea's mind every time she talked about the tree farm and how lovely it was in the winter with snow-covered branches. It was a beautiful sight without snow, in seventy-degree weather. She could only imagine what adding a few feet of snow would do.

A metal building stood off in the distance, catching Andrea's attention before they arrived at the fork in the road. The truck trundled along the gravel drive as she took everything in at once.

"That's where we have the Christmas events every year," Devon said, pointing at the building as they passed it. "Ma likes to dress up as Mrs. Claus and spend her time decorating cookies with the kids. Last time, Mrs. Langley came out and read stories. It looked like something pulled from a children's book."

Andrea tried to envision what Devon described as the "*best event ever*." She'd heard stories about it from Kate, but never in that much detail. She didn't know who Mrs. Langley was, or even what it looked like inside the building, but a part of her wanted to.

"Turn here," Devon said, pulling Andrea from her thoughts. She gasped and gripped the steering wheel, making the left turn a little too late.

"Sorry," she sputtered. "All this talk about Christmas and how lovely the event was had me drifting off to someplace else."

Devon laughed, not seeming to mind the near-miss Andrea had with an evergreen tree. "Your cabin's the second-to-last one at the end."

Andrea guided the truck along the gravel road leading to the cabins. A circular drive led them directly to the cabin deemed as hers. She couldn't believe this was where she would be staying. The view alone was incredible, but the Adirondack chairs sitting around a firepit drew her attention right away.

"Do you get a lot of guests here?" Kate had mentioned a few visitors here and there over the last few months, but it didn't seem like the place was all that busy.

"Not too many, but ever since Mya came to the ranch and worked her magic online with a website, we're getting a lot more than we did when it first opened."

Andrea pulled the truck into the empty spot next to her cabin and shifted into park, taking in the view that was going to be all hers until after the wedding.

She couldn't find the words to describe it even if someone asked her to. Everything Kate said about it hadn't painted a picture in Andrea's mind quite like seeing it for herself.

"What do you think?" Devon unbuckled his seatbelt and leaned forward, taking in the view right alongside Andrea. "It was a lot of work, but I think we pulled it off."

"Kate described it, but I didn't picture it quite like this," Andrea admitted.

"How'd you picture it?"

Andrea hated to tell him the truth of what came to mind when there was mention of a dude ranch. Certainly nothing like this. "Something a little less extravagant, maybe? Like one of those old motels—the ones you find on the side of the road hundreds of miles from anything else and in the middle of nowhere."

Devon tossed his head back and laughed. "That's what came to your mind when Kate told you about the dude ranch?"

Andrea smiled sheepishly. So what if she had an overactive imagination? Sometimes she got things wrong. Besides, she barely had time to venture out on her own. She spent most of her time focusing on racing. *The main reason for my divorce…*

She shook the thought from her mind. She wasn't going to think about that right now.

"Come on," Devon said, opening his door and hopping out of the truck. He looked back at Andrea and said, "Let's get you settled in, and then I'll show you around."

A smile pulled at Devon's lips. Maybe she misjudged his reaction to Porter suggesting that he be the one to help her get settled in. Maybe he didn't mind after all.

Andrea hopped out of the driver's seat and opened the back door. All of her belongings were nestled in cardboard boxes and strategically placed in the back of the truck. Uncertain of what the future held once her time at the ranch ended, she worried about leaving anything behind.

Devon lifted a larger box from his side with ease. "You must've packed everything but the kitchen sink."

"Pretty much." Andrea jostled a couple of boxes from the back and followed Devon to the front door of her cabin. She wondered if he would better understand if he knew that packing everything she had was her only option. "I wanted to make sure I didn't leave anything important behind."

"Apparently," Devon joked. *If he only knew the*

meaning behind my decision... "Let's set them here for now, and once we have everything unloaded from the truck, we can haul them inside."

Andrea went along with his idea, stacking boxes on the wooden porch until her truck was empty.

He fished a key from his pocket, unlocked the door, and opened it. She caught a glimpse of what awaited her inside as she rounded up a few of the lighter boxes. It seemed like a new beginning—a hopeful one—even if it was only for a few short months.

"I think Lacy mentioned more guests will be arriving later today," Devon said, carrying the heaviest box through the door and setting it down in the living room. He turned to face her, giving her a hopeful smile. "I hope you don't mind neighbors."

"I'm sure I won't," Andrea said, excited to meet new people. She enjoyed striking up random conversations with strangers and getting to know them. Everywhere she went, she liked to make new friends. Even if it ended up only being a short interaction, she made the most of it. "I get along with everyone."

"That makes one of us," Devon admitted, placing the last two boxes of Andrea's belongings on the floor next to the couch. He paused before quickly adding, "I'm not much of a people person."

Andrea studied him for a moment. She could see that. Though he was polite and followed through with what was needed, he seemed to be the type who was content with working alone.

"Well." Devon clapped his hands and looked around the room, interrupting the awkward silence surrounding them. "Would you like help putting things away, or would you rather do that later on your own after I show you around?"

"This can wait." As much as Andrea appreciated the offer to help her get everything unpacked and placed around the cabin, she would much rather take the opportunity for Devon to show her the rest of the ranch. "I'm ready."

"Alright," Devon said with a smile. "Let's go on an adventure."

Andrea's heart skipped a beat as she followed Devon out of the cabin. She was eager to see what all the ranch had to offer, especially after catching a glimpse on the way to the cabin. And hopefully, by the time Devon was done showing her around, Kate would be back from the hospital and Andrea could see her.

CHAPTER EIGHT

Devon climbed into the driver's seat of Andrea's truck, shocked she agreed to let him drive, and backed out of the driveway. He rounded the small circle of cabins and headed for the main drive that led them back to the main property.

On the way, he pointed out where everyone lived, showing Andrea each area, and anticipating any questions she might have. Though, to his surprise, she didn't say too much. Her eyes lit up as they drove through the tree farm and brightened even more when they arrived at the metal building housing the Christmas display.

He held the door open and waited for her to enter the building before closing it behind them. The building was still set up with booths and fake presents, showing a glimpse of what Christmas was like at their ranch.

"This would be perfect for the reception after the wedding," Andrea said once they finished their walk-through. She pointed to an area toward the back of the building, announcing her vision of what would end up being the highlight of the night. "We could have a food bar there, with tables and chairs set up along the walls, leaving plenty of room for dancing."

"Dancing?"

Andrea paused and turned toward him. A look of confusion spread across her face as she asked, "You do know that's something everyone expects at the reception, right?"

He rubbed a hand through the stubble on his chin and let out a light grunt. "Yeah, but—"

"Let me guess," Andrea said with a soft laugh, "you're not much for dancing either?"

He wouldn't go as far as to say that, but he supposed she hit the nail on the head and assumed correctly. It wasn't that he didn't like dancing. He just didn't know how to. But he wasn't going to tell her that. What man in his late twenties didn't know how to dance? Heck, even his youngest brother knew how to dance before he was out of diapers.

"That's okay," Andrea said, saving him from explaining his discomfort with the idea. "I wouldn't expect someone who doesn't like people to be open to dancing with them."

Well, when she put it like that, Devon couldn't argue. He could easily admit that he had given up on dancing when his two left feet caused a catastrophe on his prom night. Or, he could just as easily mention it and give Andrea a good laugh at his expense. He shrugged. *What the heck?* "I actually have two left feet, and I don't dance."

He dangled each foot out in front of him, showing off his booted feet. Andrea eyed him suspiciously and said, "I'm sure you could if you tried."

He wiggled a finger. "That's where you're wrong. I have tried, and it ended in a disaster."

"Oh?" Andrea raised a brow. "Do tell. I'd love to hear all about it."

"Let's head to the next spot, and I'll tell you," Devon said, motioning for her to follow him out of the building. He turned to face her as he opened the passenger door and pointed a warning finger at her. "If you promise not to laugh too hard."

Andrea rolled her eyes and climbed into the passenger seat. She yanked on the seatbelt, buckled herself in, and shot him a wink. "I can't make any promises."

Devon shut her door and shook his head as he made his way around the front of the truck.

As he steered the truck away from the building and guided it in the direction of Hunter and Alyssa's house, he told her about stepping on his prom date's dress, ripping it right up the side, and exposing her slip underneath. He felt embarrassed, not only for himself but for his date as well.

"At least you were a gentleman and offered to cover her with your jacket," Andrea said after a bout of laughter. Tears spilled from her eyes as she looked over at him. "I'm sure it's a night neither of you will ever forget."

Devon assumed she was right, but he'd rather forget all about that night and the heartbreak that followed. If someone would have told him high school sweethearts didn't last, he would have never taken a chance. He would have completely missed that dance and everything leading up to the heartbreak. Though he couldn't blame it on anything but being naïve. He should have known he wasn't good enough for her—the mishap at the dance had clearly been a warning sign.

"That was years ago," Andrea said, her laughing

fit clearly over. "I'm sure you could learn to dance if you just give it another chance."

When he didn't say anything, still mulling over the idea, Andrea said, "I'm sure you're not the only one who could benefit from dance lessons, you know?"

"Dance lessons?" That alone made his stomach flop. There was no way he was willing to take lessons for something he didn't care about. Besides, he wasn't required to dance at the wedding, was he? "The only ones that'll be dancing are Beckett and Kate. I'm more than okay with that."

"That isn't what Kate said." Andrea grew quiet for a minute, tapping her phone and holding it up so he could see it. Sure enough, there was a message exchange between Kate and Andrea about the reception. Right there in black and white was proof that Kate planned a night of dancing. "Unless you're planning to skip the reception altogether, I'd suggest freshening up your dance moves."

She's joking, right? He didn't plan on skipping anything—his brother would kill him. But he also knew Beckett wouldn't mind if he sat against the wall all night. Heck, Beckett would be too caught up in his beautiful bride to even notice.

"It's up to you." Andrea shrugged and tucked her

phone away. "You won't know who you'll be stuck dancing with, and I'd hate for someone's dress to rip at the reception."

It was only a slight jab. Devon could take it. He still wouldn't change his mind about dancing. He'd protest the whole idea of everyone dancing until he was blue in the face. He was *not* going to dance.

CHAPTER NINE

Andrea thanked Devon for showing her around the ranch, even though he wouldn't take her up on dance lessons. She even offered to be the one who showed him a few moves. Thankfully, she hadn't taken it personally when he politely declined her offer.

She hated to be the one to tell him that Kate planned for the wedding party to dance together. And since he was the best man… he wouldn't have a choice.

She would let Kate be the one to break the news. Speaking of Kate, she needed to finish up unboxing her things and head over to Beckett and Kate's cabin. Kate had sent her a message earlier saying that she was back home and the doctor suggested she rest for a day or two. And she needed time with her best friend.

Andrea still had a few boxes left to unpack when she decided to leave them for after her visit with Kate. Her friend needed her, and that was the main reason she was there—to help Kate with whatever she needed.

Thankfully, she found the cabin nestled in the corner of the woods without getting lost. She was proud of herself after only being shown once. If she could find her way to Kate's, then she could manage to find her way around everywhere else on the ranch.

"Knock, knock." Andrea gently rapped her knuckles on the door before stepping into the cabin. Unlike hers, Kate and Beckett's cabin was much larger in comparison. The wide-open floor plan gave a view of the gorgeous backdrop from the living room window while standing in the entryway. "Kate?"

"In here," Kate called out as Andrea saw a hand peeking over a nearby couch in the living room.

Andrea rounded the couch and wrapped her arms around Kate. "It's so good to see you. You had me so worried."

"I'm fine," Kate said, waving it off like it wasn't a big deal. "It's nothing a little extra rest and drinking water won't cure."

"What'd the doctor say?" Andrea already knew what Beckett had said, but she wanted to hear it from Kate. Bed rest was a big deal, and she knew Kate would have a hard time accepting it.

Kate sat up on the couch and patted a spot next to her. Andrea slid in next to her best friend and waited to hear the news. Planning a wedding was a major task, but she would manage it all on her own if Kate wasn't able to help. That's what friends were for. Andrea had a feeling she wouldn't be alone either way. Kate had a huge support system at the ranch and plenty of people who were willing to step in where needed.

"He says I should take it easy and not push myself too hard," Kate said, frowning. "He mentioned if I don't, he'll put me on bed rest, but I told Beckett that wasn't going to happen. The dude ranch needs me. Trail rides need to be guided, and cabins need to be cleaned."

Kate's lips formed into a soft pout. "And my wedding needs planned, and I haven't even had my dress fitting yet."

Andrea reached out and placed a hand on Kate's shoulder. "Don't worry about any of that right now. You need to focus on what matters most, and right now, that's you and this little girl."

Tears filled Kate's eyes as she looked over at Andrea. "You're such a good friend, you know that? What did I ever do to deserve you in my life?"

Andrea smiled, fighting back her own tears, knowing that her friend was having a difficult time. "I could ask the same thing."

Kate leaned into Andrea, resting her head against her shoulder. "You're the very best friend a girl could ask for. I'm thankful for our friendship."

Andrea rested her head on top of Kate's and gently squeezed her in a side hug. There weren't enough words to describe how thankful Andrea was for finding Kate when she did. At a time when she needed a friend the most, Kate was there.

"I hope everyone's been good to you," Kate said, leaning away from Andrea and looking her in the eye. "I didn't plan on ditching you."

Andrea laughed. "Of course, you didn't, but you have nothing to worry about. They've been over the top when it comes to making me feel right at home."

She hesitated before telling Kate about Devon stepping in and showing her around. She didn't want to make Kate feel worse than she already did, knowing how much she wanted to be the one to show her everything.

"Porter actually volunteered Devon to be the one

to show me around," Andrea said, keeping the conversation light and upbeat. "You should've seen his face."

"I can only imagine." Kate rolled her eyes. "Please tell me that he was nice to you."

Kate's pleading gaze made Andrea question Devon's reputation when it came to guests at the ranch. Was he really such a hermit? Though he did tell her he wasn't much for people, that didn't stop her from wondering what it was about her that changed his mind.

"Uh oh, you're silent. Tell me what happened."

Kate's words pulled Andrea from her muddled thoughts about Devon. She shook her head and offered an innocent laugh. "Oh, no, nothing happened. It was a lot of fun."

Kate furrowed her brow and repositioned herself, so she was now facing Andrea. "I can't tell if you're joking or not. Sarcasm, maybe?"

"No, I mean it. He's polite and seems to be down-to-earth," Andrea admitted, trying her best to hide the heat creeping into her cheeks. Why was she having this reaction when talking about Devon? Certainly, he hadn't had that much of an impact on her, had he? "But I'm sure he's polite to everyone, isn't he?"

Kate tipped her head back and let out a surprising

laugh. Andrea leaned forward, wanting to know what on earth Kate found so funny.

"He may be polite, but he's the most obnoxious brother here at the ranch," Kate explained, wiping tears from her eyes. Andrea was happy to see her friend laughing and in good spirits, but she was being serious. If Devon wasn't the kind of person that Andrea thought him to be, then she didn't want to spend more time with him than necessary. "He's definitely *not* your type."

Andrea sat back, slightly offended that her best friend would assume she was falling head over boots for Devon. And him not being her type... What did that even mean? "I have a type?"

Kate stifled a laugh and wiped more tears from her cheeks. *Lord, help Kate breathe through the fits of laughter bestowed upon her.* Andrea rolled her eyes. "Whatever."

"Don't get mad, Andie." Kate put on a serious face and positioned herself closer to Andrea. "It's nothing bad. We all have a type. And let's not forget that you're married."

A knot the size of a boulder formed in the pit of Andrea's stomach as Kate's eyes glanced over the bare spot on her ring finger. There wasn't anything to see but a tan line in place of what used to hold an expensive wedding ring.

Kate's eyes shot up, a look of concern clouding them. So much for not telling her until after the wedding was over. Andrea sighed. "Andie…"

Andrea bit her bottom lip, heavily regretting letting this conversation get carried away. Of course, she would have eventually had to tell Kate, but not now. She didn't want to be the black cloud on her best friend's wedding day. And, she certainly hadn't wanted to open the floodgates she'd managed to keep closed until now.

"Oh no," Kate whispered, wrapping her arms around Andrea and leaving enough space for the baby bump between them. "I'm so sorry. I had no idea. Why didn't you tell me?"

Andrea's lips trembled as she fought hard to keep the emotion from taking over. She wasn't a crier, or at least, she hadn't been. Now, it seemed she cried at the drop of a hat.

"I didn't want to ruin your wedding." Even as she said the words, she realized how silly they sounded. "I didn't want the news of my hopeless marriage ending to put a damper on you. I didn't want you to feel bad. Not when you should be on top of the world and excited for your future."

"Now I feel awful," Kate said, her bottom lip trembling as tears filled her eyes. She fanned her face with a tissue and shook her head. "Is there anything you need? I would've helped you if I would've known, Andie."

Andrea's words caught in her throat. She didn't need Kate to feel bad. It was her own fault for not telling her. She knew Kate would have done anything she could to help her through the divorce.

"I know," Andrea admitted, dabbing a tissue underneath her own eyes. "But like I said, I needed to get through it, and I didn't want to burden anyone. Especially not you."

Kate seemed to accept Andrea's explanation, though she wasn't pleased with it. Andrea knew Kate well enough to know she didn't like being kept in the dark. She didn't like surprises either. And this... was a bombshell exploding like fireworks in the dead of night.

"Are you okay?" Kate squeezed Andrea's hand as Andrea fought back the tears and swore them away. She'd thought by now she was all out of tears. Unfortunately, she was wrong yet again. She nodded, feeling anxious. "Is there anything I can do?"

Andrea dried the tears and reluctantly stared at Kate. Here she was at the ranch for her best friend's wedding, and Kate was asking if there was anything she could do for her. That wasn't how Andrea planned for this to go. "Don't worry about me. I'll be just fine. We need to focus on you. You're getting married and having a baby!"

Kate let out an exhausted sigh in response to Andrea's excitement. Andrea would worry about what she was going to do and whether she would be okay later. She had no choice but to push down the relentless emotions and get focused on planning for the biggest event of the year. But for now, she would let Kate catch up on some much-needed rest while she headed toward the barn to see her other best friend.

CHAPTER TEN

Devon walked into the main house, kicked off his boots, and hung up his hat before rounding the corner into the dining room, ready to chow down. He hadn't completed the tasks he planned to do before suppertime, but regardless of that, he'd worked up an appetite.

He joined everyone at the table, sliding in next to Mark. The ranch hand had a rocky start on the ranch, but he eventually got up to speed and proved his worth. Mark fit in with the rest of them, becoming much more like family than just a ranch hand.

Regular conversation flowed around the table while everyone waited for supper. Hunter and Alyssa talked about their latest addition to the stables and how grateful they were for the business side of things to pick up. Mya mentioned the statistics for the website, letting everyone know it was receiving more traffic than ever before. She expected them to be flooded with guests at the dude ranch before the end of the month.

Devon's father turned his attention to him, apparently waiting to hear an update on how things were going lately for him. He didn't have much to write home about. Not a lot happened where he was concerned. So, he kept his answer short, sweet, and to the point. "For me? It's the same stuff, different day."

"Well, then I'd say you're not getting out and about like you should be," his father said proudly, crossing his arms in front of his chest. He offered Devon a slight smirk, knowing Devon wouldn't argue whether he was right in his assumption. "Maybe you should spend a little less time alone and find something to occupy your time better."

"Or *someone*," Adam said with a cough.

Mya nudged him in the arm and told him to cut it out. Of course, Devon was ready for his siblings to give him a hard time. Usually, it was the other way around, and he was the one taking jabs at them when it came to relationships at the ranch.

But now, it wasn't much fun. Aside from Owen, Devon was the only one still single. Not that he cared, really. Though it would be nice to share life with someone. As long as that someone didn't mind life at the ranch and accepted him for who he was rather than who they thought he should be.

"How was your time with Andrea?" Adam asked, earning another slight nudge from Mya. Apparently, he wasn't getting the message to let it go. "Did you get her all settled in and shown around?"

With a curt nod, Devon remained quiet. He wasn't feeding into the frenzy. He knew better than to think twice about Andrea. Beckett and Kate wouldn't appreciate him dancing around the idea of him searching for a date at their wedding. Though he had heard stories of people finding their forever after attending a wedding.

He shrugged the thought away. He wasn't lucky enough to experience that kind of opportunity. Besides, hadn't someone mentioned she was married?

The back door opened as someone entered the kitchen. Devon anticipated Andrea's presence at the table, unsure why his nerves went into overdrive at the thought of her joining them.

"Speaking of Andrea," his mother said, carrying in two steaming pans of lasagna and setting them in the middle of the table. She glanced around, apparently counting heads like the mother hen she was. For whatever reason, all eyes focused on Devon. Did they really think he knew where the woman was? "Does anyone know where she is?"

"Last I knew, she was heading to Kate's place," Devon answered quickly, hoping to leave it at that. He didn't need his family thinking for one minute that he kept track of her.

"Nope, she's not there," Beckett announced from the kitchen. He pulled two plates from the cupboard and rounded the kitchen counter. He leaned against it, waiting for everyone to grab their food before helping himself. "I was just home to check on Kate and told her I'd swing by and grab food on my way back from checking on the cattle."

Again, everyone looked at Devon, assuming he knew. He hated to be the one to tell them that they were wrong in assuming anything when it came to keeping tabs on new arrivals at the ranch.

"Well, someone should look for her and invite her to supper," his mother insisted. Looking directly at Devon, she asked, "You didn't forget to invite her for supper, did you?"

"I told her," Devon stated matter-of-factly. "I mentioned it more than once."

His mother didn't seem too impressed. If she had

something she wanted to say, it appeared she wasn't going to say it.

Instead, his father chimed in. "Dev, why don't you go find her and bring her back? At least then we'll know she's okay and your mother can settle down knowing no one is going to bed on an empty stomach."

That earned Pops a playful slap from Ma as she shook her head. "You make it sound like I'm a worrywart."

His father angled himself in his chair, looking up at his mother. "You're not?"

He grunted and mumbled under his breath, "I could've sworn—"

Another swat interrupted his mumbling. "There's no swearing at the table. And besides, it's a mother's right to worry over her children, regardless of whether they're her own or not."

His father took one for the team and nonchalantly agreed to disagree.

"I don't care who goes and finds that girl, but someone needs to," his mother insisted, refusing to give up on having everyone there for supper.

Devon couldn't bear the heat of everyone's gazes for another moment. He slid back his chair from the table and stood, volunteering to be the one to find her. Even though anyone could have offered.

If he didn't know any better, it seemed his family was setting him up for something.

"Thank you," his mother said, resting a hand on his arm. "I'm sure she'll appreciate not being forgotten."

Devon nodded but didn't say another word as he tugged on his boots, grabbed his hat, and headed out the door in search of Andrea. He prayed it didn't take long to find her, because he was starving and ready to call it a night.

CHAPTER ELEVEN

Andrea relaxed in Stella's saddle, accepting the peaceful view surrounding them. She originally planned just a quick visit with her horse, but she decided to saddle up and explore the unknown. If she was going to assist in leading tomorrow's group through the trails, she wanted to at least have an idea of where she was going.

Even though Devon had shown her pretty much everything on the property from the main drive and side routes, he hadn't shown her the trails. She had enjoyed discovering more on her own.

It was getting late, and Andrea knew it had to be getting close to suppertime, but she needed this as much as she needed the air to breathe. She had agreed to come to the ranch to prepare for Kate's wedding, but the more she thought about it, it was more than that. It was an escape from everything—from her failed marriage to her conflicting doubts on what the future held, especially after her decision to retire Stella from racing.

She didn't have all the answers, but she wanted to find them. Maybe the stay at Pine Creek Ranch was just what she needed to get things figured out. Maybe soon, a door would open and lead her to wherever she needed to be.

The sunset wasn't anything like she knew from living in the suburbs. Of course, she still enjoyed taking in the view of a setting sun wherever she could, but it was different here. The sun set just beyond the mountains and provided her with a sense of peace after a long day. She could get used to something like this.

Crunching leaves behind them pulled Andrea's attention away from the stunning view. She turned in the saddle, checking behind them for signs of anyone approaching. Would the Carlson family be out looking for her if she didn't show up in time for supper? She certainly hoped not. She didn't want to worry anyone, much less become a burden when they already had so much going on at the ranch.

A low growl startled Andrea as it echoed through

the woods behind her. She knew better than to show fear, but she couldn't keep from tensing up. Of course, her reaction alerted Stella, and now she needed to regain composure for the sake of staying put in the saddle.

"It's okay, girl," Andrea said, easing the horse from the edge of the cliff and turning to face whatever was behind them. If she positioned herself carefully, they would be okay. Stella was top of the line when it came to speed, so Andrea had no doubt they could flee whatever danger approached them.

Another growl followed the sound of leaves crunching. Andrea's fight-or-flight mode kicked in, knowing if they sat here too long, whatever wild animal was growling would eventually come face to face with them.

She didn't have time to chastise herself for venturing into the woods alone. The growling animal cleared the woods and presented itself in a threatening pose, ready to attack.

Andrea's heart beat wildly in her chest, leaving her panic-stricken in fear and unable to breathe. Never in her entire life had she seen a bear in the wild, let alone knew what to do when she was confronted by one.

Stella reared, nearly throwing Andrea from the

saddle. Andrea let out a shriek, hanging onto the reins for dear life. If she fell off, there would be no way she could outrun this wild animal. She knew nothing about bears, but she did know they were fast on their feet when they were in predator mode.

Quickly, Andrea glanced around, looking for a way out. She pulled herself from a state of panic and focused on the way they'd entered the woods. If she could get Stella to focus, too, they would make it out of there.

Do I have time to get Stella to turn around and head in that direction before the bear launches at us?

There was only one way to find out. Against her better judgment, she turned Stella and spurred her in the side, praying they would make it out of this alive. The clearing was only a few hundred feet away.

The second she spurred Stella on the side, the horse took off in a full gallop, which in turn caused the bear to give chase. Andrea didn't have time to panic as she dodged tree limbs and hung on tightly to the reins.

She let out a scream as the bear neared the backside of the horse, angrily swiping every chance it could. Andrea did not want the bear to injure her horse, nor did she want the bear to get its massive paws on her.

What in the world had she been thinking? She should have known better than to go into the woods alone.

A feeling of impending doom suffocated her as they barreled through the woods. Maybe if she screamed loud enough, someone on the ranch would hear and come to her rescue. She'd seen it happen in the movies, and though it didn't seem realistic, she needed to do something.

Apparently, they had been further into the woods than Andrea thought because it was taking forever to see the clearing in front of them. She didn't have time to think about whether they'd taken a wrong turn, or if they were on the right path. She needed to stay focused on keeping out of reach, even by a hair, of the bear charging behind them.

Screaming until her throat was raw, Andrea prayed for someone to hear her. Stella wasn't slowing down anytime soon, but from the looks of it, neither was the bear.

CHAPTER TWELVE

Devon heard the screams as he stepped onto the porch. He tried his best to determine the direction they were coming from as he raced back into the house. If it was Andrea screaming, there was no telling where she might be.

Everyone had begun enjoying their meal when he entered the house and motioned for his brothers to join him. He didn't have time to explain what was happening, other than a few words about screaming coming from the woods.

His brothers ran out of the house behind him, Beckett dropping the foil-wrapped plates on the counter and grabbing a shotgun on his way out. Devon and Beckett climbed into his truck and headed in the direction he last heard the screams.

"Do you think it's Andrea?" Beckett asked, nestling the loaded shotgun safely in his lap as Devon's truck jostled along the bumpy gravel road leading them to the woods.

"I don't know who else it could be," Devon said, his focus remaining on the road in front of them. He kept his eyes peeled for signs of anyone coming out of the woods as they rounded the edge of the dude ranch. He hadn't shown Andrea the trails. He planned on joining her in the morning, knowing she didn't know the woods as well as he did. He hadn't liked the thought of her leading the group alone without being familiar with the trails into the woods. "I should've told her to stay out of the woods. I had a feeling she'd take it upon herself to see them on her own."

Beckett offered Devon a nod of agreement, but said, "Sometimes you can tell them all you want, but they'll still end up doing it. Andrea's a lot like Kate. Strong-headed and stubborn."

"Well, that might've just put her in danger," Devon said, upset and worried about what Andrea had gotten herself into.

The rest of the siblings followed Devon's truck and rounded up behind them as they neared the clearing to the woods. Devon didn't hesitate before driving straight in, making sure to take it somewhat slow not to hit anything or anyone.

"There," Beckett said, pointing to an area up ahead. "It looks like Andrea's horse."

"Is Andrea in the saddle?" Devon's heart sank. What if Andrea had fallen off the horse and was injured, unable to move? "I can't see that far ahead. Can you get a good look?"

Devon's question was answered as Andrea and her horse galloped straight toward the truck. It wasn't the panic on Andrea's face that sent Devon into action. It was the bear tagging along behind them, threatening to take them down any minute.

Devon slammed on the brakes, put the truck in park, and hopped out. Beckett rounded the back of the truck, steadying himself and aiming for the bear as it passed them—its focus solely on the prey.

A single shot echoed through the trees as Beckett pulled the trigger, readying to take another shot when the bear didn't stop. "I hit it, but it's on a mission."

Devon's eyes focused between the bear and Andrea, praying the next shot from Beckett's gun would take down the threat.

Thankfully, it did. The bear dropped to its side, letting out a low growl as life drained from it. Beckett swore under his breath as they turned back to Devon's truck. Much like Beckett, Devon hated to shoot wildlife, but sometimes they weren't given a choice. When it threatened their livestock or one another, they had to do what needed to be done.

"It doesn't look like she's stopping anytime soon," Beckett said, pointing off in the distance where Andrea was still riding Stella.

"I don't blame her," Devon said, gripping the steering wheel. He hated to think of what could have happened. He just thanked God that Andrea was safe. It could have ended tragically for all involved. "I'm sure she's going to be pretty shaken by this."

"Maybe give it a while before you lay into her about safety at the ranch, okay?" Beckett looked over at Devon, waiting for him to acknowledge what he was asking him to do. Someone needed to tell her that what she did was probably the dumbest thing ever, but Beckett was right. She didn't need to hear it right now.

Devon parked his truck near the main house and got out. Andrea was already at the barn, doubled over next to Stella. Beckett nodded for Devon to go and check on her as he headed up the porch steps. The rest of the brothers followed Beckett into the house, leaving Devon to handle Andrea.

How was he going to bite his tongue while

making sure she was okay? The fact that she went alone made his blood boil with anger. She could have been injured, or worse, the bear could have killed her.

There were dangers that the city girl should know about if she was going to be staying at the ranch.

"Hey," he called out, approaching Andrea's side. He bit his tongue, wanting so badly to tell her how stupid it was for her to go off on her own. "Are you okay?"

She looked up at him, tears spilling from her eyes, causing his anger to dissipate in an instant. He couldn't be mad at her after seeing how scared she was.

Out of instinct, he reached out and placed a hand on her shoulder. "That was a close one, but you're okay."

He wasn't much for words, and he certainly wasn't good at comforting someone—especially after they cheated death.

"I know what you're thinking," Andrea sputtered through her tears. Devon straightened, pulling his hand away from her. "I thought I could handle a ride on my own. I didn't expect to put myself or Stella in danger."

"No one does," Devon said, worried that maybe he hadn't hidden his thoughts very well. "There's a reason why we ride in pairs around here, but I wouldn't expect you to know that on your first day."

Andrea wiped angrily at the tears and rolled her eyes. "What a great first day it's been, too."

Devon let out a light chuckle, earning him a subtle glare. "What?"

"Just say it," Andrea demanded. "You think I'm stupid and shouldn't even be here."

Devon paused a moment before opening his mouth. The truth was that's exactly what he thought. Well, at least the first part. He wasn't sure how he felt about the latter yet. So far, it had been great having her there at the ranch. But that wouldn't be the case for long if she kept putting herself in danger.

"I wouldn't say that," Devon finally said with a shrug. "There's just a few things you have to know. Safety's a big thing around here."

Andrea straightened beside him, seeming to relax her shoulders. She was worked up, there was no doubt about that, and for good reason. Devon hoped it was enough to make her think twice before venturing on her own again.

"Do you see bears a lot around here?" she asked cautiously. "If so, maybe I should rethink my stay in the cabin."

Devon realized the amount of fear she felt as she

talked. How could he tell her that she would be safe in her cabin when she didn't know what occupied the woods? He knew it wasn't as easy just to tell her to play it safe. She needed reassurance.

"Well, if it makes you feel better, we haven't seen too many," Devon said. "Usually they run further up in the mountains. Kind of out of sight, out of mind."

"Until now." Andrea's voice cracked as she looked up at him.

"I wouldn't worry too much about it," Devon said, trying his best to comfort her fears. A difficult task after what she had gone through. He couldn't say how he'd feel if the shoe was on the other foot. "It's best just to be cautious and prepared for an encounter. We mainly see coyotes and a few wolves every now and then. Mostly during the colder months when they're searching for their next meal."

Andrea cringed, and he apologized.

"I'm just glad you weren't hurt," Devon admitted, feeling less angry now than what he had been. "I hate to think of the alternative."

"Me too," Andrea whispered, wiping her cheeks with the back of her hand.

"If you wanted to take a ride on the trails," Devon started, treading lightly, "you could've just asked me to go with you."

"A little late now," Andrea said, shooting him a crooked smile.

"Sorry, I guess I just assumed you wouldn't venture out on your own in unfamiliar territory." Honesty was Devon's strong suit, and he wouldn't hold back when it came to saying how he truly felt. "But then again, you seem a little rebellious."

Andrea laughed and rolled her eyes. "Hardly. I'm not one to go against the grain. I've lived by the book for years, but now, it's just…"

Her words trailed off, and Devon witnessed an expression he hadn't seen in a long time. Was it regret? Sorrow? She'd said "*lived by the book*"—past tense. What was so different now? What caused her to change?

CHAPTER THIRTEEN

Andrea spent the night tossing and turning, restless from thoughts of what could have happened in the woods. She turned on the bedside lamp and pulled a notebook from the nightstand.

On nights she couldn't sleep, it had become routine for her to pull out her journal and scribble down her thoughts. She had been to therapy the last few years, with more visits in the last few months since the divorce, but it always ended with her therapist recommending she write down her thoughts. It would help her through whatever she faced. At least, that's what her therapist promised anyway.

She glanced at the red numbers on the clock beside the bed. In less than four hours, she would be saddling up and preparing for the trail ride with a group of people she didn't know. A knot formed in the pit of her stomach at the thought of venturing into the woods again. Who was to say that she wouldn't be confronted with another nightmare while eventually leading trail rides? Would she even be able to confidently lead them?

She jotted her thoughts on the blank page in her journal, keeping pen to paper as her therapist suggested, and not stopping until she felt as though her mind was settled and a sense of peace washed over her.

Three pages later, her writing could have been the start of a book. She lightly chuckled to herself, realizing no one would want to read a memoir of her thoughts. She hardly wanted to think about them, let alone have someone read them.

It seemed ironic, really. She'd kept a diary in her teen years, dreading the thought of her parents getting a hold of it and reading what she'd written. Those words were nothing like what they were now. The pages of the journal she held in her hands and close to her heart were filled with mistakes, past regrets, and a whole lot of doubt.

At one time, she thought of herself as confident, certain of what she was supposed to do in life, knowing she had everything she ever wanted. Until she didn't.

Turning her attention back to the journal, she flipped it open to the very first page. The entry was dated less than a year ago—shortly after serving her ex-husband with divorce papers. She couldn't help but wonder what the pages would have said if she had started the journal at the first sign of her marriage failing.

Not that she needed a reminder. The reality of it still clung in the back of her mind, reminding her daily of the life she could have had—*thought* she had. She wanted nothing more than a simple life, and she had it at one time. A career that she loved, a house she adored, and a marriage she felt would last until death did them part.

How wrong was she?

It was apparent after reading several pages in the journal that she had been completely wrong in assuming life wouldn't change. She had taken so much for granted in such a short time.

She read until her eyes grew heavy, then decided to tuck the journal back in the drawer and turn off the light. She nestled underneath the blankets, praying for sleep to wash over her. Though the journaling did help her some, she still needed to settle her mind.

She thought of first arriving at the ranch. How friendly everyone had been. How welcomed she felt. To be honest, it felt like she arrived at a place she was supposed to be. It seemed foolish to think that, especially after the day she had, but there was a small part of her that truly believed it.

Her eyes drifted shut, and she welcomed sleep as she quieted the thoughts in her mind.

Less than two hours later, she woke in a panic. She kicked the covers off, frantically searching for the light next to the bed. She searched the room for any sign of a threat, relieved to find herself safe in the comfort of the cabin. She wasn't in the wilderness as she had been in her nightmare. There wasn't a bear angrily swiping at her, threatening to take Stella from her. She was alone and safe.

Once her heart calmed and the panic subsided, Andrea decided to call it a loss on sleeping for the next two hours and climbed out of bed.

Thankfully, the cupboards were fully stocked and she found the coffee right away. It didn't take her long to make a pot of coffee, knowing she would need it if she was going to get through the day.

It was just after five when the coffee pot beeped, letting her know it was coffee time. She planned to drink two cups before showering and heading out for the day. She wanted to stop by Kate's first before heading to the dude ranch and meeting up with the group of trail riders.

She could only hope that Kate wouldn't hop to her feet and tell Andrea that she would be the one leading the group. Andrea might be stubborn, but Kate beat her by a mile.

Andrea didn't want her friend overdoing it, but she certainly wouldn't mind someone coming along with her during the trail rides. But who else could she ask to join her? And would that mean she had to admit she was afraid?

Deciding now wasn't the time to worry about it, Andrea finished drinking a cup of coffee and went about her early-morning tasks of getting ready. Maybe if she showered and got ready in time, she could drink her coffee on the porch and watch the sun come up. But only if the coast was clear. The cabins were surrounded by woods, and she didn't want to encounter anything wild for the rest of her time at the ranch—not even if it was something smaller and less aggressive than a bear, like a raccoon or a deer.

With her hair haphazardly wrapped in a towel, Andrea made her way back to the kitchen. Living in a cabin was a luxury compared to the apartment she was used to. She had plenty of room in the bathroom, not to mention the wide-open floor plan of the cabin itself. There was a lot of space unclaimed, leaving her to wonder what she would fill it up with if it was her own someday.

She poured herself another cup of coffee, noting that she was somehow already on her fourth cup—even though she'd only planned to drink two. Hopefully, the caffeine would keep her energy up and not plummet shortly after getting the day started.

Andrea carried the cup of coffee, along with her journal, to the sliding doors at the back of the cabin. The sun was just beginning to rise on the east side of the property, giving her time to settle in and relax in its warm rays as she wrote a few lines on a blank page.

She paused mid-sentence at the sound of something rumbling nearby. Normally, she would have shrugged it off as her stomach, knowing it was getting close to breakfast time. But this was a different rumbling. Not loud like thunder, but loud enough to distract her from her thoughts.

No sooner had she heard the noise than it disappeared. It must have been someone passing through. She needed to calm down and realize there wasn't anything to fear that she hadn't already faced. What could be worse than a bear wanting to kill her?

Heavy footsteps echoed behind her through the cabin, and for a minute, she froze. Not wanting to turn around, she tried to imagine she was just hearing things. There might not be anything worse than a bear, but someone entering her cabin without permission was a close second.

"Good morning," a familiar voice called out over her shoulder. She relaxed in the chair and let out a relieved sigh. So, it wasn't a bear or an unwelcome stranger. It was Devon. "I was just passing by when I saw your lights on. Figured I'd stop and ask if you're up for some breakfast."

Andrea quickly closed her journal and rested it on her lap as she glanced over her shoulder. Devon stood behind her, offering a foil-covered plate. He shrugged with a grin and said, "Ma figured it might be too early to expect you at the main house, so she had me bring it to you instead."

Devon carried the plate of food as he made his way around the patio furniture and set it down on the glass table by Andrea. He glanced at the journal in her lap and said, "I hope I'm not interrupting anything. I just saw you sitting out here when I knocked on the front door."

Of course, the wide-open floor plan she liked had its disadvantages, too. Someone standing at her front door could see almost everything throughout the cabin.

She glanced down at her journal and quickly set it to the side. "Oh, no, not at all. I was just enjoying a cup of coffee while watching the sun come up."

Devon looked out toward the vast spread of trees. "It's quite the view, isn't it?"

Andrea had to agree with him. She hadn't seen anything like it. Living in the suburbs, surrounded by tall buildings in Dallas, Texas, didn't leave much of a view for anything else.

"When we built these cabins, that's one thing we wanted to make sure to include," he said, glancing around, seeming proud of his family's accomplishment. "I haven't met one person who doesn't enjoy watching the sun rise and set."

Andrea nodded. Of course, wanting to watch the sunset, among other things, had been the reason she'd found herself in danger yesterday. But she didn't tell him something he couldn't care less about.

"Anyway," Devon said, shifting in his chair. "I hope you don't mind that I'll be joining you on the trail rides today."

Andrea nearly choked on her coffee. She set the cup down next to the still-wrapped plate of food and looked at him. Did he think she couldn't handle it after what happened?

"Not because I don't think you can handle it," he said, clearly reading her thoughts. "But because I need to get Buck out for a while, and there's no better time than now."

She wanted to believe him, but she struggled a bit. But, then again, hadn't she told herself that she wouldn't mind someone else joining her? She cleared her throat. She just hadn't thought it would be him.

Instead of questioning him, she focused on Buck, who she assumed was his horse. "Buck?"

Devon ran a hand down the back of his neck and chuckled. "Yeah, Buck got his name when he first arrived at the ranch. I purchased him at an auction, thinking he would've made a great roping horse, but instead, he turned out to be better at bucking."

"Why do I sense there's a good story behind that?" Andrea said, drinking the last of her coffee.

"Why don't you go ahead and finish getting ready, and I'll tell you all about it on the way to the barn?"

Devon stood from his chair and slid on his cowboy hat. She couldn't argue with his suggestion, though she still didn't like the thought of him not trusting her to lead the trail rides on her own. But then again, he did tell her that no one does anything alone around the ranch. So he was probably just joining her for safety reasons, right?

She thought about refilling her cup on her way to fix her hair, but she decided she'd probably had enough coffee for now. Besides, she wanted to hear all about Devon and the horse who proved him wrong.

CHAPTER FOURTEEN

Devon hated to admit what he thought when he first saw Andrea wearing a towel on her head. She looked good, despite her hair being tangled in a knotted towel and not a trace of makeup on.

He'd let his thoughts carry him away while he waited for her to finish getting ready which, to his surprise, hadn't taken her long at all. And despite him not wanting to be attracted to her, she was stunning. He mentally kicked himself to remind himself that she was happily taken and he shouldn't be interested.

"Ready?" he asked, biting his tongue to stop from telling her what he truly wanted to. He didn't need to tell her that she was beautiful. She probably heard that several times a day anyway… from her husband.

"I'm all set," Andrea said, pulling on her cowgirl boots before clapping her hands. "I'm ready to hear all about this horse of yours."

Devon reached for the door and held it for her as she walked past. How had he forgotten in such a short time that he promised to tell her about Buck? He shrugged as he closed the door behind them.

He met her at the passenger side of his truck and opened the door, waiting patiently for her to climb in and get buckled in before rounding the truck to the driver's side. If she had a problem with riding in his truck, she hadn't mentioned it. Maybe he'd been wrong about her. Maybe she didn't care about shiny, expensive things.

Devon steered the truck out of the driveway and guided it down the gravel road. He had less than three minutes to tell her about Buck, and maybe within that time, she would get a good laugh. She seemed tense this morning, and after what happened yesterday, he couldn't blame her. But the last thing he wanted was for her to dwell on it and not enjoy her time at the ranch.

"After paying a pretty penny for him, I brought him back to the ranch," Devon started, keeping his eye on the road. He continued when Andrea looked at him, wanting to hear more. "Right away, Hunter told me I made a huge mistake."

"Why's that? There's no way he knew the horse was trouble before unloading him, right?"

"Wrong," Devon said with a grin. "Hunter knows horses better than anyone here. He didn't even have to spend a whole minute with Buck to know he was going to be a pain in the butt."

Andrea seemed to accept his answer, so he continued with his story. "It wasn't long before I realized Hunter was right. That horse gave me a run for my money."

Before they arrived at the barn, he finished his story by telling her about how his horse had changed. From troubled and inattentive to relaxed and more confident, thanks to Hunter.

"Hence why he earned the name Buck," Devon stated matter-of-factly. His horse had bucked him off so many times that he lost count, and still to this day, depending on Buck's mood, there was a chance he'd revert to his old ways. "But Hunter's a miracle worker when it comes to horses. Same as Alyssa. You know she stepped in when Hunter stepped out?"

Andrea shook her head. "I don't know much about the dynamics here, other than what Kate has told me."

"And she hasn't mentioned any of the past drama?" Devon grunted. Apparently, Kate hadn't told her about the goings on at the ranch which, in his opinion, was a reason to stick around. There was never a dull moment where his family was concerned. "Not that there's a lot that happens around here, but when it does…"

His words trailed off when he caught a distant look in Andrea's eyes. Maybe she didn't care to hear about their family dynamics. He should probably change the subject.

He pulled the truck in next to the barn and shifted into park before climbing out. Andrea remained silent, seeming lost in thought, but he decided to let it be. Hopefully, he hadn't said anything to offend her… which would be a first for him. He scrubbed the back of his neck. *Since when do I care if I offend anyone?*

"How about you get Stella ready while I focus on Buck?" Devon suggested, closing the passenger door and following Andrea to the barn. "It might take me a good while to get him ready. I'm not sure if I've mentioned it or not, but our time together lately has been few and far between."

She stopped near the barn's entrance and turned to face him. "Do you think it's a good idea to take him along with us?"

"Don't think it would hurt anything to get him out," Devon said, knowing Andrea had good reason to be concerned. "He'll adjust."

"And if he doesn't?"

Why was she doubting his abilities to manage his own horse? It wasn't his first time riding the darn thing. He and Buck went way back, for years. He hadn't been a month past turning sixteen when he decided he needed to invest in a horse. He wanted to be like his older brothers at the time, and they each had a horse of their own. Heck, even his twin brother, Beckett, had one of his own.

Apparently, Andrea didn't have an answer. Instead, she flashed a quick smirk and walked into the barn.

What was it about her that stirred something inside of him? He shook it off and blamed it on himself for letting things get to him. He knew better than to take things personally. A person couldn't maintain a ranch while letting emotions get in the way.

There was something about her. He just couldn't put a finger on it.

He entered the barn behind Andrea, watching as she made her way to the end stall where her horse awaited her. He enjoyed watching the interaction between the two, wondering what made Andrea decide to quit racing. She'd mentioned retiring the horse, but from what he could see, the horse wasn't even that old. She certainly had a few more good years of racing left in her.

Shrugging it off, Devon approached Buck's stall. He regretted taking time away from his horse and not giving him the attention he deserved. Of course, Hunter and Alyssa looked after him when Devon got busy fixing things around the ranch, which honestly, was a never-ending cycle. There was always something to fix—a fence needed to be mended, the equipment needed new parts. The list went on with more things added to it daily than Devon cared to admit.

"Hey, bud." He greeted the horse, placing his hand over the stall door and giving Buck a scratch on the side of the neck. "What do you say we go for a long ride today?"

Buck nudged against the door, impatiently waiting for Devon to open it and let him out.

"Settle your horses," Devon chided, unlatching the door once he grabbed the reins from a nearby hook. When Buck nudged the door again, Devon gave the horse a stern look. "Patience there, Mr. Bucky."

Devon was just getting around to placing the saddle on Buck when Andrea and her horse strode past the stall. He sensed she was showing off, making a point about his horse and trying to get him to second-guess taking Buck along for the ride.

He tightened the straps and led Buck out of the stall, clearing the barn before calling out to Andrea. "Are you going to wait for us?"

"If you can catch up." She smiled back at him, a competitive shine in her eyes.

He grunted as he climbed into the saddle. Andrea and Stella were already way ahead of him, but he knew Buck had it in him to catch up. There wasn't anything his horse couldn't do, or at least he hoped, anyway.

They came to a stop near the entrance of the dude ranch where families and their children gathered. He expected Andrea to boast about her win, but judging by the look of unease resting on her face, that wasn't going to happen.

"What's wrong?" Devon asked, sidling up next to Andrea. "That's not the face of someone who just won a race."

"I didn't expect there to be kids here," Andrea stated flatly.

"Yeah, so?" *Does she not like kids?* Devon couldn't see what the big deal was.

Andrea shot him a worried look. One that told

him her concern was legitimate and not something to shrug off. "I don't know if I can do this."

"You're backing out?"

She shot him a glare, letting him know he probably shouldn't have asked that. But he needed to know. If she didn't want to go on the trail, he would have to find someone else, and quickly.

"After what happened yesterday…"

With just a few words, he knew. It wasn't that she didn't like kids. She was fearful of what could happen. If it could happen to her, it could happen again, and she didn't want them to get hurt.

"It's okay," he said, fully understanding her fear. "I'll be right here the whole time. I won't let anything happen, and neither will Alyssa, who is also going with us."

Andrea inhaled a deep breath and released it slowly. He could see the worry weighing on her shoulders. He didn't want to pressure her into doing something she wasn't comfortable doing, but he had no doubts that she could do this.

"Do you want me to go in front of you?" He offered just for the sake of offering, but if it made her feel better about it…

"No, it's okay." She sidestepped with Stella next to him. Glancing at the crowd, Andrea's eyes filled with concern once again. "I just don't want anything to happen. What do we do if it happens again?"

"It won't. I promise."

He kicked himself for promising something he had no control over. But he knew what happened yesterday had been a fluke—something that had never happened at the ranch. They'd only had to shoot two wild animals that he knew about. And that had been over the course of several years. It wasn't something he expected to happen regularly.

"So, what do you say? You lead in front with Alyssa, and I'll head up the rear?" Devon shot her a quick smile, letting her know it would be okay.

To his surprise, she agreed and led them toward the group gathered at the dude ranch. He kind of liked knowing that she trusted him and the fact that he could put her worries at ease. That's about as far as he was willing to take it, no matter what his attraction had to say about it.

CHAPTER FIFTEEN

The trail ride went smoothly. There was no sign of any random bears wanting to cause chaos, and the children following her seemed to enjoy the ride. From what she gathered from the parents, most of these kids had ridden before, and they were there to round out the last of their summer activities before heading back to school.

Andrea felt a sense of pride wash over her as they headed back to the dude ranch. She had only gotten a glimpse of what the trails had to offer yesterday, and she was thankful for the opportunity to see more.

It helped that Devon had come along with her. If he hadn't been there, who knew if she would have been able to follow through with her task to help lead the group through the woods and further along the trail.

Devon smiled as he climbed out of the saddle and planted his feet on the ground. The children were ready to cool the horses down as they were originally instructed, but Andrea had a feeling most of them just wanted to play in the water.

"You did good," Devon said, walking over to where she stood next to Stella. She busied herself with the task of cooling Stella down, knowing her horse wasn't used to long rides, even though it was good for her—and for Andrea as well. "I'm proud of you."

Her heart senselessly skipped a beat at his words. She tucked a loose strand of hair behind her ear after removing her helmet. He was proud of her. It wasn't just his words that sent her heart into a frenzy, it was the way he was looking at her.

"Thank you."

"I'll finish up with this group and send them on their way," Devon offered, hitching a thumb over his shoulder. "We can decide what to do next after getting the horses back to the barn."

"Okay," she said. She couldn't wrap her mind around Devon wanting to make an entire day out of this. *Does he really want to spend that much time with me?*

She enjoyed the trail ride and liked having him there with her, but didn't he have other things to do at the ranch? Surely, there had to be fences to mend or required repairs. If he thought he needed to do her any favors by spending extra time with her, she would have to be the one to tell him otherwise.

The trail ride was fun, and though Andrea liked the feeling of being carefree and participating in fun and games, she knew it wouldn't be long until she had to focus on what she was there for. Kate needed help with the wedding. Even though she had spent plenty of time on the phone with Kate, going over details for the wedding, there were still things they needed to discuss.

And Kate had mentioned her dress. There was a chance her wedding dress no longer fit, and Andrea wanted to make sure and cover all bases. If Kate needed a new dress, they would have to spend time shopping for one. Not to mention the bridesmaid dresses and groomsmen's tuxes.

Andrea glanced around, trying to picture the wedding-to-be. The barn toward the back of the dude ranch, deserted and not occupied by extra horses, would soon be hosting the main event. From where she stood, she could already tell there were a lot of things needing to be done with it. Of course, Kate wanted the wedding there and Andrea wouldn't argue with that. It had the potential to be the most beautiful attraction of the wedding, aside from the bride.

Andrea wondered what Devon would say when she told him that he would need to fix a few things. Would he be as willing to repair an old barn as he was to join her on a trail ride? She highly doubted it, but she could use all the help she could get if she wanted Kate and Beckett's wedding to turn out just the way Kate dreamed it would.

"Please don't tell me you're looking at Devon like that," a blonde woman said, approaching Andrea's side. She had yet to meet everyone, including the woman who just pulled her from her thoughts. "I'm Mya, by the way."

Andrea accepted the woman's hand and smiled. "Nice to meet you."

"Same to you, but I'm really hoping that you weren't looking at Devon," Mya said, glancing over her shoulder to where Devon was standing and instructing the group of children. "He's single, but he's also the last one I expect to get married around here. And that says a lot considering Owen is still up for grabs."

Mya laughed, but Andrea felt unsettled by the brash assumption. She had been staring off in the distance, but not at Devon. She had been looking at the barn behind him. But judging by the fascinated look on Mya's face, she wouldn't take Andrea's word for it.

Mya lifted a pail of cleaning supplies and said, "Anyway, I just finished cleaning the cabins, and I'm about to head to the main house to see if there's anything Diane needs help with. Want to join me?"

As much as Andrea wanted to say yes, she hesitated. She looked over at Devon, this time locking eyes with him. He shot her a wink that sent her heart into overdrive and heat creeping up her neck. If she planned on denying her attraction to Devon, there was no sense in doing so now. Mya clearly witnessed what his wink had done to Andrea.

"Unless you have other plans," Mya whispered, stifling a laugh as she nudged Andrea. "I wouldn't want to interrupt anything. I'm sure Diane will insist there isn't anything she needs help with, and I'll be back to work on the website."

Before Andrea could give her a definitive answer, Devon approached them. "Hey, Mya. How are things going?"

"They're going great," Mya said, holding the pail

up. "I was just seeing if Andrea wanted to tag along to the main house, but she said she already made plans with you."

Andrea nearly choked on air as she tried her best to tell Devon that wasn't true. She had mentioned no such thing. A soft smile pulled at his lips as he looked from Mya to Andrea. She didn't have the heart to tell him now.

"Well, in that case, we should get to it," he said. How dare he go along with what Mya said. Even if it was partially the truth.

Mya waved and parted ways, sending a quick wink at Andrea before turning her attention back to the path in front of her.

"It's okay if that's not what you told her," Devon said, pulling Andrea's focus back to him. She quirked a brow, wondering how on earth he knew her so well already. "You'll realize soon enough that my family, and their significant others, have a thing for setting everyone up around here."

Andrea swallowed the lump in her throat. *Is that what Mya was doing? Trying to set me up with Devon?* Come to think of it, perhaps it hadn't been just Mya. Even yesterday, Porter suggested Devon be the one to show her around the ranch. And Kate—her best friend—insisted that once she arrived at the ranch, they would have to work with Devon to get things fixed up in time for the wedding.

"And it's okay if you don't like me," Devon said with a shrug, though Andrea could tell it might bother him not to be liked. "A relationship is the last thing on my mind. I wouldn't mind being single for the rest of my life."

Is this the part where she should tell him there was no chance that she would act on her attraction to him? Did he even suspect that she was attracted to him? He was observant, she'd give him that—especially when it came to reading her expressions like a book.

"If you want, you can head to the main house with Mya. I'll get the horses back in the barn now that everyone's taken off for the day." He rubbed the back of his neck, something he seemed to do a lot. "I'm sure I'll find something that needs to be fixed around here before lunch is ready."

Making light of the most awkward situation, Andrea said, "I'm sure I've already found something."

Devon raised a brow. "What's that?"

Andrea nodded toward the vacant barn and waited for Devon to catch on. He let out a low groan and shook his head. "Nope, not doing that."

"But it needs to be fixed up," Andrea insisted, knowing that's what Kate wanted. She'd heard her friend mention this barn more times in the last two months than she'd ever heard her talk about anything else. "Kate has big plans for that barn, and we have to follow through with it."

"We?" Devon furrowed his brow. She wasn't sure he could get more attractive than he already was, until now. "Who's this *we* you're referring to?"

Andrea played it off the best she could, but he still wasn't giving in.

"That barn has been that way since... well, forever," Devon stated matter-of-factly. Andrea had guessed right. He wasn't as willing to do this as he had been for other things. "My grandparents owned this ranch for a lot of years before passing it on to my father, and my great-grandfather owned it before them. Who knows how long that barn has been standing. I'm not going to be the one to ruin history."

Andrea held back a laugh. *He's kidding, right?*

"I mean it," Devon said, crossing his arms in front of his chest. "If that's where Kate wants the wedding, then she needs to accept it how it is."

Andrea's jaw dropped. He really wasn't willing to budge. "But that's where Kate and Beckett first met back in high school. A lot of memories were made in that barn, and she wants to reminisce about them on her wedding day."

Nope, he still wasn't budging.

"I'm sure there were plenty of memories made in that barn." His sarcasm killed her. This was not how she expected the conversation to go between them. "Like I've already said, that barn has been standing for a half century or more. I'm not changing it for anything, including my brother's wedding."

She awkwardly shifted her focus away from the sore spot, not sure what to say now that he made it perfectly clear he wasn't willing to fix up the barn.

So much for him keeping the title of *Mr. Fix It*.

CHAPTER SIXTEEN

Devon hadn't planned to leave Andrea back at the dude ranch, but he was ticked off. There was no way he was going to touch that barn, especially knowing how much it had meant to his grandparents at one time.

He was sure that he would get an earful once the news traveled and Beckett caught wind of it, but he would tell him the same thing he told Andrea. He wasn't going to let some barrel-racing diva waltz onto the ranch and demand things be fixed at their family's expense. That went for both Kate *and* Andrea.

He blew out a frustrated breath and kicked the fence post. That conversation could have gone a million different ways, but of course, it had to end on a not-so-pleasant note.

"Easy there, bro," Beckett said, approaching Devon's side. "What'd that fence ever do to you?"

"A lot of things," Devon said sourly. "If I have to mend this darn thing one more time—"

"You're going to bulldoze it?" Beckett tipped his head back and laughed. When he realized Devon wasn't joking around, his face fell flat. "What happened?"

Devon debated on whether or not to tell Beckett the gist of his most recent conversation with Andrea. What would his brother say when he realized Devon wasn't willing to do what needed to be done? He'd made a promise to Beckett to do whatever he needed to do for the wedding. He knew this wedding was a big deal to Beckett. Even though he had yet to figure out why weddings were such a big deal anyway. Statistics proved that nearly half of all marriages ended in divorce, and he imagined those numbers would continue to climb.

No one worked out their problems anymore. They would rather bob and weave to ignore them instead of facing them head-on. Relationships weren't like they once were, that was for sure. If Devon was going to settle, he wanted to make sure it was with someone who was willing to fight for what they had and not give up at the first hurdle.

"This doesn't have anything to do with Andrea, does it?"

"No." Devon was too quick to answer. Beckett knew him better than anyone else. His brother more than likely already put two and two together and had Devon all figured out.

"You were just fine this morning before the trail ride," Beckett said, pointing out the obvious. Devon let out another frustrated sigh and removed his hat. He ran his hand through his sweat-matted hair and looked back toward the spot where he'd left Andrea standing with her horse. He wouldn't blame her if she never spoke to him again. But then again, maybe that was for the best. "Thought so. Are you going to tell me what happened, or should I just wait for it to come through the grapevine?"

Devon grunted and put his hat back on, angling it to keep the sun out of his eyes as he went back to work on the fence. He had a feeling Beckett wouldn't let it go until he told him what he wanted to hear, but for right now, he needed to let out his frustration with hard labor.

"I can tell that you like her," Beckett said. Aside from the bellowing of nearby cattle, his brother interrupted the much-needed silence. "If she's anything like Kate, which she is, she's not going to budge without a fight. So, whatever the two of you are spatting about, you might as well give in and do whatever you have to do."

Devon was not going to do that. He didn't care if that's what Beckett did for Kate. He wasn't going to be the one to bend. Especially when it came to the ranch.

"I don't like her." It wasn't exactly true, but it felt good to say it. Maybe if he said it a few more times, he'd believe it.

"Is it about the barn?"

Devon paused from tightening the wire around the fence post. Leave it to Beckett to hit the nail on the head with his first guess. Not that Devon considered it guessing. Beckett just knew things. Much like their father and their brothers. They all had a strong sense of when things weren't right with one another.

"You have to let it go and move on," Beckett said, taking his tone down a few notches. "I had a feeling it was going to upset you when Kate told everyone that's where she wanted to have the wedding ceremony."

Devon grunted, cranking on the wire and twisting it around itself.

"Maybe working on it would help get your frustrations out," Beckett offered. Even though his brother had a point that it might help, Devon wanted nothing to do with it. He would find another way to forget the past. It wasn't like Beckett would understand. His high school sweetheart came back to him. Not to mention Kate never once said Beckett wasn't good enough for her. "Do you know the number of proposals that fail?"

Devon didn't care. "Probably the same amount that marriages do."

Beckett tipped his head side to side. "I'll give you that one, but seriously. Think about it. So what if your ex said no and left you high and dry? You're better for it. Imagine if you ended up with someone who truly wasn't happy being with you."

"Thank God I haven't," Devon mumbled under his breath.

"Do you want to know what I think?" Beckett shifted his weight, leaning against the fence. Whether Devon wanted to or not, Beckett would say it anyway.

He shrugged. "You can say whatever you want. It isn't going to change my mind."

Before Beckett had a chance to say anything, he was interrupted by Mya. "Hey, Dev, where's Andrea? I thought the two of you had plans."

Devon grumbled under his breath. "Here we go. Why can't I just have some peace and quiet for once without anyone asking me where the newbie is?"

Beckett let out a laugh and slapped him on the shoulder. "I'll talk to you later. I've got to check on Kate. Make sure she isn't doing anything she isn't supposed to."

Devon tried to pretend like he hadn't heard Mya. Of course, that didn't stop her from asking him for a second time. He straightened away from the fence, biting his tongue and doing his best to curb his anger. He didn't want to take his frustrations out on the wrong person—especially when it was his own dang fault.

"Did you leave her at the dude ranch?" Mya asked when Devon didn't say anything. "Everything okay?"

"Yeah, everything's perfectly fine," Devon said through gritted teeth. "I've got to get this fence fixed. She had something else going on."

Mya raised a brow, clearly calling his bluff. It was stupid of him to lie. He wasn't good at it, and apparently, everyone could see right through him. Maybe Beckett was right. Maybe he needed to chill out.

"Okay, well, I have this stack of magazines that I think Andrea and Kate would enjoy looking at," Mya said, not realizing that Devon had already moved on and his focus was back on the fence. He couldn't care less what Mya had, especially if it involved the wedding. He needed to take a step back from it all and give his thoughts a break.

If only his mind would get the memo. Since leaving Andrea at the dude ranch, he couldn't stop thinking about how everything went down. He was a God-fearing man, and he was raised to treat women with respect. The way he reacted wouldn't make his father proud. Heck, it didn't make him feel too good, either.

"Are you sure everything's okay?" Mya asked again, still not convinced. "If this fence is giving you trouble, I'm sure Adam wouldn't mind—"

"It's fine." His tone was a bit sharp, but he wanted to be left alone.

Mya took a step back and held the magazines tightly to her chest. "Okay, I guess I'll talk to you later?"

Devon felt awful for being short with everyone who mattered to him. Not that his short fuse was anything new. It was something he had been working on.

To be honest, he was handling it well until that

blonde-haired, blue-eyed beauty pulled into the ranch and sent him into a tailspin. He wasn't one to fall head over boots for someone he barely knew, and he didn't believe in all that *love-at-first-sight* stuff, but he also couldn't find another explanation for how he felt about Andrea.

CHAPTER SEVENTEEN

Since she hadn't touched the plate of food Devon brought over this morning, Andrea pulled off the foil and slid the plate into the microwave. She had no idea what Devon's connection to that barn was, but she wouldn't touch that live wire again. She would let Kate handle that one.

Thinking of Kate, Andrea debated on whether to visit her once she finished eating. Deciding that was what she would do, she sent a message to Kate letting her know she would be there soon.

It didn't take long before she found her way to Kate's place and knocked on the door before slowly entering the cabin. If Beckett was there, she planned to leave them be and come back another time.

But rather than finding Beckett sitting beside

Kate, she saw Mya. She offered a friendly wave, greeting them both as she entered the living room and sat in a recliner across from them.

"Beckett told me what happened. Are you okay?" A concerned look crossed Kate's face as she looked over at Andrea. "I'm sorry. I should've told you not to go alone. You never know what's out there in the woods."

"I know that now," Andrea said, offering a sheepish grin. "I'm just thankful the guys came to my rescue."

"I hate to think about what might've happened if they hadn't." Mya cringed and shook with a shiver. "That's something Adam made sure I knew when I first came to the ranch."

Andrea couldn't blame anyone for not warning her. It should have been common sense. But after living in the suburbs, surrounded by tall buildings and heavy traffic, she hadn't given it a second thought.

"I also heard what happened today with the barn," Kate said, folding her hands in her lap. Andrea raised a brow, wondering how she would know. But with one look at Mya, she put it together. Mya must have overheard the argument. "Don't worry. It wasn't anything personal. There are a lot of memories tied to that barn. I'm sure Devon isn't the only one who doesn't want it touched."

Andrea shrugged. "Wouldn't they want to restore it? Keep it standing? I mean, it's weathered, and it's the perfect spot for the wedding ceremony. I don't understand what the big deal is and why Devon…"

Her words trailed off as Kate and Mya exchanged looks. Okay, so maybe there was something to it that she didn't know. Either way, it wasn't any of her business.

"I'll talk to Devon about it," Kate said. "He doesn't take too well to change. Especially when us 'outsiders' start pointing out areas on the ranch needing updates."

Mya agreed with a nod. "Adam's the same way."

"I think all of the Carlson brothers are to some extent," Kate explained, making Andrea feel a little better about butting heads with Devon. It wasn't anything personal. But if it wasn't, then why did she feel like it was? "I'll see if Beckett wants to talk to him about it. Maybe we'll leave that to the brothers."

"I think that's a great idea," Mya said, leaning forward and reaching for a stack of magazines. "Us girls can figure out everything else. Like wedding colors and centerpieces."

Mya had a dreamy look in her eyes as she flipped

through the first few pages of a magazine. Andrea's stomach knotted at the thought of going through with planning the wedding. *Can I really do this? Is it too much too soon?* There was no doubt in her mind that she was thrilled with her friend's soon-to-be wedding, but what if Andrea couldn't be the chipper, upbeat bridesmaid Kate was expecting her to be?

"I cannot wait to do this for my wedding," Mya said, sporadically flipping pages. Kate lifted a magazine from the stack and flipped it open. Andrea followed suit, not wanting to be the odd one out.

"Are you getting married soon?" Andrea asked, glancing at Mya's left hand where a beautiful diamond ring glinted back at her.

"We're still figuring out everything, but I think it'll be sooner rather than later," Mya said. Her eyes lit up as though a thought crossed her mind. "Maybe you could help me plan my wedding, too?"

Andrea looked at Kate, who seemed lost in her own world while skimming through the magazines. She hadn't thought about what she would do once Kate's wedding was over and her work at the ranch was complete. Could she stick around and plan weddings for a living?

"Don't worry," Mya said, interrupting Andrea's thoughts. "It won't be until after Christmas. Winter and holiday months are super busy and expensive around here. I don't want to put more pressure on the ranch during that time."

Andrea nodded, not sure why Mya would want her help with her wedding. She barely knew her. But no sooner had the thought of being a stranger crossed her mind than she remembered Kate's words. *"Everyone's going to love you. There's no such thing as strangers here. Diane always says 'The more the merrier.' You'll fit right in with the rest of us."*

They spent nearly two hours going through magazines and discussing the final details, including colors, bouquets, and centerpieces. It wasn't until Kate mentioned wine tasting and needing to find a caterer big enough to feed everyone at the reception that Andrea realized there was a lot still left to figure out and not much time to do it.

"I'm sure if we reach out to Pine's Wine and Dine, they'll be able to accommodate everything we'll need," Mya suggested, leaving Andrea thankful for the suggestion. She didn't know the town well enough. She'd originally planned to have Kate show her around, telling her the ins and outs of the small town and what all it offered. "They have the best food, and obviously the best wine as well. Adam took me there recently, and it was an amazing experience."

Kate seemed to like the idea as her lips pulled into a smile. Andrea would go along with whatever Mya suggested if Kate approved. She couldn't shake the feeling of being the odd one out, though, no matter how warm and inviting everyone seemed.

"I also overheard Mrs. Langley telling Diane she'd love to bake for the wedding," Mya said, keeping her focus on the overwhelming details. Andrea's head was spinning with the laundry list of to-dos.

"Maybe we could invite her for coffee sometime at Sunrise Café and go over the details," Kate said with a smile. "I know she loves to join in on social events around town. She makes the best chocolate chip cookies. I'm sure she has recipe cards full of appetizers and snacks we can serve at the wedding."

"I like that idea," Andrea admitted. "I'd love to meet her."

"We can see if your mom has time to help as well, Kate," Mya said. She turned to Andrea and said, "I don't think there's anything Ruby can't do. She owns the small jewelry store downtown, and she enjoys getting involved in her spare time."

Everything seemed to be falling into place. What had once been an overwhelming thought was now becoming something more manageable. Andrea hadn't told Kate how she truly felt about planning a wedding, especially since her focus was on doing what needed to be done to help her friend. It didn't matter that planning weddings wasn't her area of expertise, did it?

She certainly hoped not. She didn't even plan her own. She had hired an overly expensive wedding planner to handle everything for her. Aside from breaking the bank, Andrea didn't have anything to worry about.

If only I had known how it would end, I could have saved a fortune.

"Okay"—Kate clapped cheerfully—"I've got an idea. How about we head into town? We can even grab a bite to eat, but not before I show you my dress."

Andrea watched as Kate stood from the couch and made her way to the bedroom at the back of the cabin. She almost questioned whether her friend should do anything against her doctor's orders, but knew that Kate had a mind of her own.

Kate returned a few moments later carrying her dress. It was the ideal blend of reserved and modern—something that fit Kate perfectly.

Or at least, hypothetically. Kate struggled into the dress, crying out when she realized her baby bump was hindering her attempt at fitting into the dress. Andrea's heart dropped the second Kate's smile faded and tears welled in her eyes.

"I bought this dress long before receiving news that we were expecting," Kate said, blubbering through uncontrollable tears at this point. Andrea and Mya tried to comfort her, telling her that it wasn't a dealbreaker. "I'm going to look like a beached whale on my wedding day."

Andrea stifled a laugh, knowing full well it wasn't funny, but she couldn't help it. "That's not true at all, and you know it."

Kate wiped at the tears staining her cheeks. "I might as well just wrap a king-sized sheet around me at this point. There's no way I can find another dress."

"I'm sure we'll be able to find you something," Mya chimed in, looking as perplexed as Andrea felt. *How are we going to find a dress in this short amount of time?* "Maybe we could stop by and see Addy?"

Andrea raised a brow, wondering who Addy was. She didn't know the town all that well, but she didn't recall seeing a dress shop or boutique on her way to the ranch.

"Okay, let's go," Kate said, turning toward the door and sliding her sandals on. "I'll pray that someone miraculously donated a beautiful wedding dress to the thrift store."

"And maybe a few bridesmaid dresses as well," Mya said cheerfully as they made their way out of the cabin and to Kate's truck.

Andrea had no problem shopping at a thrift store, but what were the chances they would have what Kate was looking for? She appreciated Mya's optimism, but she silently prayed for an answered prayer as she climbed into the cab of the truck.

CHAPTER EIGHTEEN

Devon spent the rest of the afternoon focusing on mending fences around the property. Adam and Beckett were in the west pasture herding the cattle to give Devon a little time to get the fences up to par.

Thankfully, by the time his brothers rolled in with the herd, he'd completed the task. Now, he needed to figure out what else needed to be done. At least if he kept his mind preoccupied with the tasks at hand, he wouldn't think about Andrea and the apology he owed her.

"Thanks for fixing the fence," Beckett said, climbing out of the saddle with Adam in tow. His brothers stopped near the edge of the fence line and exchanged a look. "These cattle have wreaked havoc in the west while waiting on us to bring 'em over here."

Devon knew what that meant. The west pasture needed a break, and the herd would be putting his mending skills here to the test, not to mention adding another thing to his plate when it came to checking on the fence line along the west side of the property.

"Mya mentioned helping you with the barn," Adam said, climbing out of his saddle and approaching the fence. "If you're looking for help, I wouldn't mind pitching in."

Beckett waved a hand underneath his chin in a slicing motion, trying to let Adam know it was a sore subject. Devon appreciated his brother's attempt at cutting Adam off, but he didn't need to worry. He wasn't going to blow another fuse at the mention of the barn. He spent most of the day thinking about it—and how wrong he had been to blow up.

"I'll take you up on that," Devon said. Beckett's eyes widened at the realization of what Devon said. Devon nodded, confirming Beckett heard him right. "I think the old barn could use some much-needed TLC. It's been standing for a long time, and I know I'm not the only one who would like it to stay standing."

Beckett exchanged a look with Adam, and they agreed with Devon.

"Just so you know," Beckett said, resting his arm on the fence post. "I'm sure there are going to be plenty more memories made in that barn for years to come."

"Maybe." Devon didn't really want to think about it. He was just glad that he came to his senses and realized he didn't need to get so worked up over it. Whether the barn served more memories or not, he couldn't care less.

"When are you planning to start working on it?" Adam raised a brow and glanced over his shoulder as Kate's truck drove by. Three women smiled and waved, catching Devon off guard. Andrea locked eyes with him as her smile faded. "Where are they going?"

Beckett shrugged. "Beats me. Probably doing some girly stuff together. Kate's feeling a lot better than she was, and I think it'd do her some good to get out of the house for a bit."

Devon wasn't listening to the conversation between his brothers. He was focused on the reaction Andrea had at seeing him. He really needed to get his butt in gear and come up with a good reason to visit with her. At least by then, he would have an apology at the ready and know exactly what he was going to say.

"Hey, bro," Adam called out, nudging Devon on the shoulder. "Did you hear me?"

Devon turned his attention back to his brothers and shrugged. "No, I guess not. What were you saying?"

Adam repeated what he had said to Beckett about the barn and the spare time he would have on his hands now that the cattle were in the west pasture. He would have a few days to help wherever Beckett and Devon needed him.

"Sounds good," Devon said, still not one hundred percent focused on the conversation. "I'll let you know."

With that, his brothers took off toward the horse barn and left Devon to figure out what he would do next. He had plenty of time before eating supper with the family, so he decided to venture out to the old barn.

He made his way to the barn and approached Buck's stall. The horse had done fairly well with handling the group of trail riders, along with the ride itself. Devon had made a mental note to get his horse out of the barn more often, and there was no better time than now.

"Ready to go for another ride, boy?" He scrubbed a hand through the horse's mane, scratching the area Buck liked scratched the most. The horse nudged him, letting him know he'd had enough scratching for now. He was ready to ride. "Okay, settle down."

Devon placed the saddle on Buck's back and tightened the straps. Once he had the reins in place and Buck accepted the bit, it was time to head out of the barn.

The ride to the old barn went smoothly, though he didn't really expect it to go any other way. Every now and then, however, the horse got a wild hair, which kept Devon on high alert.

"Easy, boy," Devon coached the horse, slowing him down as they approached the weathered barn. From the looks of the outside, it wouldn't take much to fix it up. He would need to replace a few rotten boards, slap on a few coats of fresh paint, and then focus on updating the wiring. He couldn't remember the last time he'd seen the barn lit up, but it was something he looked forward to.

He tied Buck off to a nearby tree and walked into the barn. Memories of the night he'd proposed crossed his mind as he stood in the exact same spot. All he'd wanted back then was someone to join him on this crazy thing called life. He'd thought Nicole was the one, but as Beckett had said, Devon should be happy with how things ended up.

Devon should be thankful she hadn't agreed to marry him. But no matter how many times he'd told himself that things worked out the way God planned, his bruised pride and punctured heart wouldn't hear him out. Rejection hurt.

To be honest, that was the main reason he'd steered clear of dating in recent years. He didn't want to face rejection more than once. A few of his brothers might think he was taking the easy way out, but Devon didn't agree. It was difficult to stand by while everyone else found the one they could spend the rest of their lives with.

Spending time with the kids during the trail ride made him realize what he was missing out on. He tried to imagine what life on the ranch would be like if he had a wife and kids. What would change if he found someone worth settling down with.

The question was, was he even ready to settle down? He'd been single for so long, regardless of the fact he was only twenty-five, but years weren't slowing down anytime soon. Before he knew it, he'd be old and gray, and the thought nearly took him out.

He laughed to himself as he glanced around the barn. Cobwebs hung in every corner of the abandoned barn. He still couldn't see what Kate did when it came to making this the venue for the wedding, but to each their own. If it was something she and Beckett wanted, who was he to question it?

Devon went back out and checked the side walls, walking the perimeter in weeds to his knees. They would certainly need to mow and weed eat, and apply a gallon or two of bug spray before the day of the wedding. He hated to think of the number of mosquitos hanging around, let alone chiggers and every other biting insect there might be.

Maybe once he met with Andrea, after he apologized, he could tell her about his plans for the barn. Until then, he would make mental notes on what needed to be fixed first.

CHAPTER NINETEEN

"I can't believe Addy knew just what we were looking for," Mya announced happily as they sat in a booth along the bay window at Sunrise Café. The diner was quaint and perfect for a quick bite to eat while they talked about their visit to the thrift store. "And let's not forget to thank God for her knowing someone who could hook a girl up with the perfect dress for her wedding day."

They clinked their glasses over the table. Andrea had settled for a cup of coffee, feeling the effects of multiple recent restless nights of sleep. Mya and Kate ordered root beer floats, which made Andrea question her drink of choice. The ice cream mixed with root beer looked so good. Maybe she would order one once she finished her round of coffee.

"I like the thought of Addy partnering with her aunt's business," Kate said, tipping her head back in satisfaction after taking the first drink of her float. "I think this town could use a little boutique. And Addy would be the ideal person to run it. She has so much expertise when it comes to fashion and design. I would shop there until I was broke."

"I agree," Mya said, placing a spoonful of ice cream into her mouth. She pointed the spoon toward the top of her cup and looked at Andrea. "Are you sure you don't want to try this? You have no idea how good it tastes."

"I'll order one in a minute, but thanks anyway," Andrea said, politely turning down Mya's offer. "Did Addy mention how long it would take the dresses to come in? If she did, I wasn't paying attention."

"I think she said it could take a couple of weeks, but the turnaround for alterations could possibly take longer," Mya said, recalling the conversation they must have had with Addy while Andrea was elsewhere. Mya looked at Kate, who seemed lost in heaven with her dessert. "Hopefully, we won't need to worry about that. I'm sure ordering up a size like Addy suggested will give that little girl of yours plenty of room."

Kate scooped another spoonful of ice cream into

her mouth and nodded. "Is it foolish of me to hope I'll need it tucked in rather than extended a mile by the time my wedding day rolls around?"

"I'd say that's wishful thinking, but you never know," Mya said with a slight shrug. "Either way, everything's going to work out just like it should."

The waitress approached the table and smiled at their conversation. "Your wedding's coming soon, isn't it? Diane mentioned something about it the other day. I've always imagined what having a wedding in the fall would be like."

Kate glanced up and smiled. The waitress was in her younger twenties, and from what Andrea could tell, there was no engagement ring on her finger. Perhaps the young woman was simply hopeful, dreaming of the day she said "*I do*."

"Are you ready to order, or would you like a few more minutes?"

Kate looked at Andrea and then at Mya. All three of them were ready to order. Andrea stopped herself from ordering everything on the menu. The breakfast food she'd eaten earlier in the day hadn't kept her satiated—especially now that it was late-afternoon and she had skipped lunch.

The waitress took their order and promised to return with Andrea's root beer float. She took Mya's word for it and had no regrets when she took the first bite of ice cream mixed with root beer. The sugary treat was just what she needed after enjoying a day out in the late-summer sun.

"See? I told you they were good," Mya said, gloating that she had been the one to talk Andrea into getting one for herself.

Andrea thanked her while quietly enjoying the late-afternoon treat. After the day she had, she gladly accepted the comfort food—and her meal was just that. The waitress brought heaping plates of everything the three of them ordered and set them down on the table.

"This looks amazing," Andrea said, her mouth watering from the aroma of carbs waiting for her to devour. She missed home-cooked meals, and aside from Diane's cooking, she knew exactly where she could find them now. Maybe when she didn't feel like eating with the Carlsons, she would venture into the cozy diner.

Thirty minutes later, fully stuffed, and ready to head back to the ranch, Andrea appreciated the time she had spent with Kate and Mya. She was thankful for the new friendship she'd found with Mya while reminiscing about her friendship with Kate. New friendships were always the best, especially when they came at a time when Andrea needed it the most.

"Now don't be surprised if Diane is upset that we're not making it to supper," Mya announced as Kate pulled the truck into Andrea's driveway at her cabin. "She doesn't like it when we skip meals around here."

"But I'm sure she'll understand when we tell her why," Kate added with a smile. "She'll be happy to hear that we found what we were looking for in town today. I'll make sure and tell her all about it when I stop at the main house to grab Beckett."

On that note, Andrea climbed out of the truck and waved goodbye to her friends. She felt thankful for the opportunity she'd been given to come to the ranch long before the wedding. Her heart was full of happiness and cheer, and she couldn't wait to write in her journal about it. She was certain her therapist would be thrilled to hear the good news and how well things were going in Pine Creek—even if it started out a bit rocky.

Andrea had the virtual visit down in her phone's calendar and couldn't wait to meet tomorrow. It had been a couple of months since she last spoke to her therapist, and this time, she wasn't dreading it.

The cabin seemed much larger now that she was

alone, making her wish she had someone to spend her spare time with. If only she could have Stella at the cabin with her. Instead, her horse was clear on the other side of the ranch. Granted, she could see her anytime she wanted, but what were the chances she would run into Devon on her way there? He seemed to be everywhere she looked, even though she would rather not see him ever again. The argument they had earlier was uncomfortable and completely unexpected. She'd been wrong to assume the two of them would get along without conflict.

Not to mention the attraction she felt igniting between them. The lingering gazes and subtle touches had been enough to signal something was stirring between them.

Oh well, it's probably best if I lie low for a while anyway. Maybe Kate would mention everything to Beckett, and Beckett would take the matter into his own hands. If his brother was the one to tell him the barn needed to be fixed up for the wedding, then Devon might not get so heated about it.

Andrea grabbed her journal from the nightstand beside her bed and walked back into the living room. She settled on the couch and put her feet up. Opening the journal, she read over the last entry she wrote, and she was surprised at how nervous she'd felt prior to the trail ride.

She couldn't help but wonder if that fear would have subsided if it hadn't been for Devon's offer to join her.

She flipped the page, eager to forget all about her encounter with the bear, as well as the disagreement with Devon. She clicked her pen and began scribbling notes about her day, thankful to have brought the journal along with her instead of burning it like she originally planned to do before arriving at the ranch. She would be mortified if anyone found her journal and read what was written in ink inside.

CHAPTER TWENTY

"Are you at least going to take her a plate of food?" his mother asked, clearly realizing that Devon was avoiding the inevitable of seeing Andrea again. Heck, even he knew it wasn't going to happen. Everywhere he looked, there she was.

Granted, it had been almost a week since he'd last seen her—since their argument right after the trail ride. He wouldn't argue the fact that he shouldn't have put off apologizing, though it was the one thing pestering his mind lately.

"Someone needs to make sure she's getting plenty to eat," his mother carried on, dishing food from the pan onto a plate before wrapping it with tin foil. "I know Kate and Mya have said she's been enjoying the food at the diner, but I'd still like to make sure she's doing okay."

He could argue with his mother. He could straightforwardly tell her if she was so worried about Andrea, she could just as easily take the plate of food to her instead. But that wouldn't do him any favors.

"Go on, son," his father chimed in, flipping through the newspaper absentmindedly. It was something he did every evening after supper. His father barely skimmed the page before flipping it, leaving no room for doubt that he wasn't reading it. "It wouldn't hurt for the two of you to make amends, anyway. You can't tell me that you don't care or that you don't like her. It was obvious the day she arrived. That girl nearly knocked you off your feet."

Devon laughed it off, letting his father's words roll in one ear and out the other. His father was full of it. There was no way Devon had been knocked off his feet when he first met Andrea.

"Can't deny the spark I've seen between the two of you," his mother said, apparently enjoying the moment as she handed him the plate of food. "I don't care what you say to her, just make sure she knows we don't want her to feel left out."

"I'm sure she already knows," Devon said, fighting the urge to roll his eyes. He accepted the plate of food, regardless of wanting to avoid it. His mother was unrelenting when it came to getting what she wanted, and if she wanted Devon to take Andrea a plate of food, he didn't have a leg to stand on. "But whatever. I'll make sure she knows this was your idea."

His mother patted him on the cheek and smiled. "Tell her whatever makes you feel better. I'm just doing my job and keeping everyone in line around here."

With a warm plate of food in his hand, Devon left the main house and climbed into his truck. So much for avoiding the inevitable. Not that he didn't want to apologize to Andrea, but there was something telling him it would be better to leave it be.

He shrugged it off, placing the plate in the passenger seat and turning the key in the ignition. His old truck fired up on the first try, though he wished it hadn't. Then he would at least have an excuse not to carry out his mother's wishes.

Devon gripped the steering wheel as a knot formed in his stomach. What was he going to say when Andrea opened the door and realized it was him standing on her front porch? Would she slam the door in his face? He wouldn't really blame her if she did.

He guided the truck along the gravel road leading

to the dude ranch and inhaled a deep breath before releasing it slowly. He could do this. No matter what his fight-or-flight mode was telling him to do, he knew he needed to at least tell Andrea that he was sorry for reacting the way he did. He needed to apologize for his short fuse and maybe, if she let him, he could explain his reasoning for acting the way he did.

Not that he was looking for an excuse. That wasn't it at all. He'd made enough excuses in his life to make up for his lack of control when it came to his temper. He needed to own up to it and face it head-on. The last thing he wanted was for Andrea to think of him as a jerk.

Shifting the truck into park, he killed the engine and contemplated the choices he had. He could back out of the drive and head for home, then tell his mother that he did in fact deliver the food to Andrea and once again realize what kind of terrible liar he made. Or, he could walk right up to the door and offer the apology he had put off until now.

It didn't take long to decide he needed to do what was right. He stood on the doorstep and knocked, steadying his breathing while thinking of what to say if she decided to let him in.

Andrea peeked out of a nearby window, a blank expression on her face when she noticed he was the one knocking on her door. Even though it took her a minute to open it, Devon was thankful to hear the lock disengage before Andrea appeared in the doorway.

He held up the plate of food and asked, "Are you hungry?"

Of course, that wasn't what he'd planned to say. He silently kicked himself when Andrea looked down at the foil-wrapped plate and shook her head. *Now what am I supposed to say?*

"Sorry, but I just got back from having supper in town," she said, glancing up and meeting his eyes. "But thanks, anyway."

Devon scrubbed a hand over the back of his neck. "Alright, that's fine. I told Ma there was probably a good reason you weren't at supper with us. But you know how she is. Wanting to make sure no one's left out."

He was stammering like an idiot. He needed to stop while he was ahead. Just accept the fact she wasn't taking the plate of food and turn around and leave with his tail tucked between his legs.

The awkward silence between them was almost too much, but he didn't know what to say. Instead, he stood there like an idiot, holding an unwanted plate of food and staring at her. Was he waiting for her to say something? No, the ball was in his court. He needed to make the first move. That's why he was there in the first place, right?

"Hey, look," he started, still not sure how this would turn out. "I want to apologize for the way I—"

"It's fine," Andrea said, seeming to wave it off like it hadn't been that big of a deal. "I get it. The barn means something, and you don't want to mess it up."

Is this the part where I need to explain myself? It wasn't that he thought it would mess it up. That wasn't the case at all. It was something more… but he didn't know how to describe it. *Will she even understand if I try?*

"That's just the thing," Devon said, praying for the words to come out right. "I shouldn't have reacted the way I did. I had no reason to get that worked up over something like that. And for that, I'm sorry."

Andrea raised a brow, most likely thinking he was an idiot. Not that he could blame her. But that's not how he wanted her to think of him. He might have a short fuse, which he was working on, but that didn't make him any less of a gentleman. He had a big heart, and he cared deeply about what his actions did to others. Well, at least, recently anyway.

Andrea reached out for the plate, and he handed it

to her. "I can warm this up later or tomorrow if I get hungry, I guess. Thank you for bringing it."

Wait. What is happening?

Maybe this was his cue to exit stage left.

He nodded and turned to leave. He was at the first step when Andrea called out to him. "Have you had supper? I might've lied a little. I haven't eaten yet, but this is a lot of food for one person."

He shook his head. Even though he'd joined the family at the table, he really hadn't eaten all that much.

"Want to join me? It gets pretty boring here by myself," Andrea said, holding the plate up. "I could use some company."

Devon entered the cabin, kicking his boots off by the door. If Andrea wanted company, who was he to turn her down? To be honest, he could use some company himself. It had been a long week without interacting with much of anyone at the ranch.

He slid into a chair at the table, waiting for Andrea to divvy up the heaping plate of food between them. She set a plate in front of him and smiled. "Your mom sure has a way to get what she wants, doesn't she?"

"You have no idea." Devon hated to think about it, but Andrea was right.

"Kate mentioned how upset she gets when people skip meals around here," Andrea said, stabbing a piece of chicken with her fork. "I just didn't think she'd send the guard to my place."

Devon laughed, stuffing a bite of barbeque chicken into his mouth. "You think I'm the guard?"

Andrea offered a slight shrug. "It's possible."

Devon tipped his head back and laughed once more. If she thought he was the guard, she was wrong. William, being the oldest brother, was the guard. Everyone else was a peasant. He laughed at the prospect of it.

They ate in silence for a few moments until he decided to clear up the misunderstanding about the barn.

"You know, it's quite foolish the way I reacted about that old barn," Devon started, taking another bite of food from his plate. Andrea shot him a look that told him he didn't need to go there again, but he ignored it. "Just hear me out. I already know it's going to sound ridiculous, and who knows what you'll think, but Beckett made me realize I needed to let it go."

Andrea raised a brow, clearly interested in hearing what he had to say. She continued eating while he told her about his failed proposal. How, for so many generations, that barn and the area surrounding it, had been the ultimate place to propose.

Only when he got to the part of being turned down did he realize Andrea had stopped eating and was now looking at him with pity in her eyes.

"Don't look at me like that," Devon said, pointing an empty fork at her. "I can't take the pitiful look you're giving me. It was bad enough to be rejected. Now I have everyone feeling sorry for me."

Andrea frowned. "But that's so sad. I can't imagine the heartbreak you must've felt."

Devon shrugged, playing it off like it wasn't a big deal. "It doesn't hurt when you don't have a heart."

Andrea's laughter echoed throughout the dining room, causing Devon to lean back in his chair and cross his arms over his chest. "What's so funny about that?"

"What are you the Tin Man from *The Wizard of Oz*? You have a heart, and you know it," Andrea pointed out. "You just wear it on your sleeve whether you want to or not."

Devon quirked a brow and leaned forward, sliding the empty plate to the side and resting his arms on the table. "So you're going to refer to me as the Tin Man? Who are you, then, Dorothy?"

Andrea shook her head, stifling a laugh as she stared him in the eyes.

"Do you have ruby red slippers around here somewhere? How many times have you clicked your heels and pleaded that *there's no place like home*?"

"Unlike Dorothy, I'm not sure where home is," Andrea said, her smile fading into a frown. Devon didn't know what to say to that, so he just waited for her to explain. "And even if I did have the famous ruby slippers, I'm not sure where I'd end up."

Devon heard the emotion in Andrea's words. He didn't have to read her facial expression to know how she felt. "What makes you say that? Don't you have a huge house back in the city where you and your husband live?"

Andrea's gaze lifted from her half-eaten plate of food and studied him. There was a hesitation in her eyes, and he had no idea what she was going to say next. He glanced down at her left hand, oblivious until now that she wasn't wearing a wedding ring. A fading tan line took its place. He had no idea. In fact, he couldn't figure out why anyone hadn't mentioned it.

Andrea followed his gaze, landing on her bare finger. She offered a half-hearted smile and shrugged. "I guess I don't have to explain now, right?"

Devon choked on the lump in his throat. What a way to stick his foot in his mouth. "I'm sorry. I only knew what Kate said about you, and she never once mentioned that you were no longer married."

So much for not feeling like an idiot. Over one hurdle just to be hit by another one.

"She didn't know either," Andrea said, a look of disappointment filling her eyes. He stared into them, wondering how on earth she hadn't told Kate. Wasn't Kate her best friend? He didn't know much about girls and their friendships, but he assumed there wasn't anything not talked about. "I didn't want to tell her because I was afraid it would ruin her mood for the wedding. I didn't want her to feel sorry for me and not celebrate her big day like she should."

"Does she know now?" Devon wouldn't be the one to tell Kate, but he still wanted to know if Kate knew. He couldn't imagine it ruining the moment for Kate. His brother and Kate had a great thing, and though he knew Kate would feel bad, he couldn't see her putting off the wedding just because a friend's marriage failed. But what did he know? Maybe Kate would fear the same thing happening to her. He had no idea what went through women's minds.

"Yes, and she told me how silly I was for not telling her," Andrea said, folding her hands in front of her. "I see that now, but I still didn't want to take the chance of it ruining her perspective of getting married. Not all marriages end in divorce."

"Most of them do," Devon blurted, failing to bite his tongue. He slapped a hand over his mouth and quickly apologized. When Andrea's lips pulled into a half-smile, he shrugged and said, "At least you're not alone?"

She tossed a used napkin across the table at him. "Gee, thanks. Way to make a girl feel better."

"I try." Devon grinned through his regret. "I'm sorry that you went through that. I barely handled rejection during my proposal. I'd hate to think about how I'd react if faced with divorce."

Andrea shrugged. "I couldn't stay with him after what he did. He didn't give me a choice."

Silence surrounded them at the table as Devon debated on whether to ask what happened. Did he really need to know? If Andrea wanted him to know, she would tell him. It wasn't his place to dive into her personal life.

"Our marriage faltered long before he cheated anyway," Andrea said, in an effort to be transparent. "And it wasn't like I didn't try to save it. I quit racing and everything to prove how much I wanted it to work out. I guess it wasn't enough, and he'd already moved on to the next in line."

Devon was flabbergasted as the missing pieces fell into place. He had wondered why Andrea retired Stella from racing so early in her career. It hadn't made sense at the time, but now, it was perfectly clear. She'd given up her career as a barrel racer to save her marriage. Except, her sacrifice went unnoticed.

If he had someone like Andrea in his life, willing to do whatever it took to save their relationship, he wouldn't shrug it off as if it were nothing. That right there was commitment. Something he wanted in a partner. Something he valued more than anything else in a relationship.

"Are you okay?"

Andrea nodded, taking back the napkin she had thrown at him, and dabbed her eyes. He wanted to reach out and tell her that what she did to save her marriage was commendable, but instead, he sat in disbelief that someone didn't think twice about losing a woman like Andrea.

CHAPTER TWENTY-ONE

After accepting Devon's apology, and telling him about her divorce, Andrea had a new respect for him. He might have a quick temper and a short fuse, but he was kind hearted and a true gentleman. When he explained the reason behind his frustrations about the barn, she understood wholeheartedly. She understood the barn was a sore spot, and it didn't help that he'd been rejected.

The two of them were complete opposites when it came to certain things, but at the end of the day, she noticed a lot of similarities. She didn't believe in love at first sight, or give much thought to insta-love, but she did believe in connecting with someone on a different level.

She didn't need to rush into another relationship, aside from the fact that wasn't what she was looking for at the ranch. But there was no denying the attraction she felt toward Devon.

"I heard that Devon brought you supper last night," Mya said, opening the door to the metal building housing the Christmas decorations. Andrea was grateful for Mya's offer to help get the place cleaned out. Sure, they still had a little over a month before the wedding followed by the reception, but Andrea wanted a head start. Otherwise, she'd find herself lost in thoughts of what life would be like if she stayed at the ranch and things transpired between her and Devon. "Tell me everything. Don't you dare leave anything out."

Andrea grabbed a stack of wrapping paper and shoved it into a plastic tote. She found a few empty totes in the loft above them shortly after searching for something to put the decorations in.

"Nothing happened," Andrea admitted. "He came over, apologized for reacting the way he did about the barn, and we talked."

"*Talked*, okay. If that's what they call it nowadays." Mya carried a large, wooden present to the side of the building and placed it along the wall. "I know it hasn't been very long, but I also know what I see when I'm around you guys."

"And what's that?" Andrea laughed it off as she helped Mya carry more wooden presents and stack them along the wall. "Please, enlighten me."

Mya rolled her eyes and wiped the sweat beading on her forehead with the back of her arm. "This is going to take forever."

"What? Telling me what you see? That shouldn't take too long since there's nothing to see."

"Not that." Mya let out a sigh and shook her head. She waved her arms at the decorations still crowding the space. "*This*. It's going to take a lot more help than just the two of us if we want to get this place ready."

Andrea hated to admit she might be right. They had already spent most of the morning clearing what Andrea thought to be most of it. It pained her to know she had been wrong. They still had several booths, random decorations, and now totes full without anywhere else to store stuff. Not to mention the sleigh parked in the back of the building. She knew without a doubt that Kate wouldn't want that to be the focus of her reception.

Even though the sleigh was neat. Each wooden slat seemed to be carved and carefully designed. She wondered how the family acquired such an extraordinary piece to include in their very own winter wonderland.

"Porter built this," Mya said, as though she read Andrea's thoughts. She ran a hand along the edge of the sleigh and smiled. "The brothers helped out when they could, but Porter did most of the work himself."

She turned to face Andrea and said, "You should see his woodshop sometime. You'd be amazed at what he's currently working on."

Andrea had no idea Porter enjoyed woodworking. Was there anything that man couldn't do? He seemed to be a jack of all trades at the ranch, much like someone else she knew when she thought about it. Devon seemed to have acquired a knack for working on things as well. *Did he get that from his father?*

"We could take a break from this, and I can show you," Mya suggested, taking a step back from the sleigh. Andrea wasn't sure about taking a break. If they stopped now, who's to say they would get everything done in time? "Come on. It'll be fun. We can finish up once you see the shop."

Andrea couldn't pull back her hand as Mya grabbed it and tugged her along. She would be lying if she said she didn't want to take a break from the never-ending shuffle happening in the Christmas department.

She followed Mya from the building and across the gravel road separating them from the administration building and the small shop attached on the side. Mya glanced over at Andrea and pointed to the shop's entrance. "We can go in over there."

"Will Porter mind that we're going in there?"

"Of course not. He likes when people inquire about his work." Mya held the door open as Andrea walked into the not-so-small shop. Wooden projects lined the floorspace, and it was obvious this was how Porter kept himself busy. "Believe it or not, he actually made most of the furniture for the dude ranch, including those Adirondack chairs around the fire pit."

Andrea had no idea, but she could see that. The table in her cabin had a unique quality she wouldn't find in the name-brand furniture she was used to seeing. There was something special about handmade furniture.

"What I'm about to show you has to be kept secret," Mya said, pressing a finger against her lips. "You can't tell Kate. It's a surprise."

Mya held out a pinky finger, and Andrea locked

hers around it, honoring the age-old pinky promise between friends.

Mya led Andrea around a few pieces of furniture until they stopped next to something square covered by an oversized sheet. Mya's eyes widened with excitement as she glanced back at Andrea. "Ready?"

Andrea nodded, completely speechless when Mya pulled back the sheet and displayed the work of art underneath it.

"It's going to be the best present ever," Mya said, clapping her hands and smiling. "Kate has no idea, and Porter's been working on this for months. He was upset that he missed the deadline of Kate's baby shower, but I told him that he still had plenty of time and not to worry. Kate's going to love it."

Kate was going to love the wooden crib. There was no doubt about it. It was obvious that Porter had spent a lot of time working on it and was in the process of sanding it down. With just a few more hours of sanding and staining, the crib would be ready for Kate's little one.

"Porter loves doing things for everyone," Mya explained. "Porter and Diane go above and beyond around here, and it doesn't go unnoticed by any of us. We all appreciate them dearly. The ranch wouldn't be what it is without them. They take everyone under their wing and don't bat an eye when it comes to helping."

An emotion Andrea hadn't felt in a long time crept into the pit of her stomach. If this is what Porter would do for Kate, she couldn't imagine what else he would do for those he loved. He was the epitome of how a father should be. Her father would have never gone out of his way to gift her with anything, much less build it. Which was why she no longer talked to him. After losing her mother, she cut ties with him and didn't care to tell him one word about her divorce. Somehow, he would have made her feel like it was her fault the man she loved and vowed to marry had cheated on her.

"This is incredible," Andrea whispered, pushing back the tears that threatened to escape. "Kate's going to be thrilled when he gives this to her."

Mya nodded in agreement before returning the sheet how they'd found it. The door behind them opened, and to Andrea's surprise, it wasn't Porter who entered the shop.

"What are you doing?" Devon asked, looking from Mya to Andrea. He furrowed his brow and ran a hand over the back of his neck. "Neither one of you can tell Kate. That's Pops's surprise for her and the baby. You can't say a word."

"I won't," Andrea promised, feeling guilty for being caught red-handed. "It's okay that we're in here, isn't it?"

Tearing her gaze from Devon, Andrea looked to Mya. She couldn't tell whether he was upset or not. Mya didn't seem affected by his presence. Instead, she laughed and told Andrea to relax. Maybe guilt wasn't the cause of the butterflies in her stomach. Maybe it was the way Devon had looked at her when he first walked in.

"I've been working on something, too," Devon said with a grin. "Want to see it?"

Mya glanced at her wrist and feigned surprise. "I just remembered I have to upload some pictures I took the other night to the website."

She headed for the door, turned back to face Andrea, and said, "I'll meet you back at the Christmas displays in an hour?"

"Sure," Andrea said, trying to figure out why Mya wanted out of there so fast. She turned back to Devon, who offered a sheepish grin. "What?"

"Nothing," he said, motioning for her to follow him over to the corner of the shop. "I've been working on this set of rocking chairs for my front porch. It's taken me a while, but I just finished them the other day. I figured I'd finish up on my own projects before getting started on the barn."

Andrea let the question of why he would need two chairs to flee her mind. He lived alone, but maybe he just wanted an extra one for company. That made sense, didn't it? Besides, who was she to care how many chairs he had sitting on his front porch?

The butterflies were relentless as she approached Devon's side. The subtle hint of cologne caused her senses to kick into overdrive, no matter how badly she tried to ignore it.

"What do you think? Want to take them back to my place and try them out?"

Was he asking her to ride back to his place just to test out the chairs? She really needed to get back to work on the building across the way if she had any hope of finishing it before losing her umph.

"Or you can get back to whatever it was you were doing," Devon said with a shrug. "There's always another day."

Did she want to put off spending time with him? He was right. There would always be another day. Cleaning and emptying out the Christmas displays could wait. If she didn't know any better, there was a reason why Mya had left in such a hurry—so Andrea and Devon would be alone.

"Sure," Andrea said with a smile, giving in to temptation. She could use a much-needed break from cleaning anyway. And what better way to do that than sitting in rocking chairs and enjoying the view? "Do you want my help loading them into your truck?"

She could almost see the excitement dancing in his eyes at the mention of going with him. Was he looking forward to spending time with her just the same as she was with him?

Waiting for her cue to help, Andrea watched his arm muscles bulge in his tight-fitting T-shirt as he carried a chair toward the door. He looked back, catching her mid-stare, and smiled. "You can stand there looking pretty. I'll do the heavy lifting."

Well, in that case, Andrea would do just that. She didn't mind the view, and to be fair, she didn't feel like lifting and carrying anything heavy either. She was sore after spending hours working with the Christmas decorations.

She followed him out of the woodshop and waited for him to place the second chair in the back of his truck. He closed the tailgate and walked around to the passenger side, opening the door, and motioning for her to hop in.

Once they were on their way, Andrea cut through

the silence in the cab of the truck. "How many wood projects have you made?"

Devon offered a humble shrug and glanced over at her. "Not as many as Pops, but I've completed a few."

Andrea waited for him to tell her what they were, but soon realized he wasn't going to. At least not without a slight nudge. "What were you working on before these chairs?"

He looked at her, awakening the once-settled butterflies in her stomach. There was something in the way he looked at her that sent her reeling. Was Mya right when she said she had seen something in the way Devon looked at Andrea? Was it that obvious to everyone but her?

"I'll show you when we get to my place." He said it so confidently, there wasn't room to question whether he wanted to tell her. A part of her anticipated seeing his work while the other part of her questioned whether it was good to spend uninterrupted time alone with him.

She looked at him in a different way after their conversation the other night. She'd felt vulnerable, and he'd made her feel acknowledged, listened to—something she had yet to experience with a man.

"What are you thinking about?" Devon asked, not

only pulling her gaze from him, but her mind as well. "I can see the gears turning. Pretty soon I'll be seeing the smoke coming from your ears."

Should I tell him the truth? That she felt comfortable being around him. That he made her feel a way she'd never felt before. He would probably laugh and tell her she'd lost her mind. But then again, wasn't he just as vulnerable that night with her?

"Just thinking about the other night," she admitted. She offered a shy smile, almost reluctant to see his reaction. His lips turned into a slight grin as he pulled the truck in next to his cabin.

"Oh yeah?" He shut the truck off and turned to face her in the seat. "What about it?"

Her heart beat wildly in her chest. This was the moment of truth. She'd already said too much, and there was no backing out of it now. Unbuckling her seatbelt, she turned in the seat to face him. She inhaled a deep breath and released it slowly, willing herself not to worry about anything. *Just be honest and see where it goes.*

"I really enjoyed our conversation, is all," she said shyly.

"I did, too," Devon said, resting his hands in his lap and focusing on her. "I feel like we somehow connected on a deeper level."

"You did?" She wasn't sure why she was questioning it. Didn't she feel the same exact way?

"Of course," Devon said with a nod. "It's not every day that I open up to someone and tell them about my past. I don't casually talk about my feelings, in case you haven't noticed, but I felt like I could do that with you. And I think… if I'm not mistaken, you might've felt the same way when talking to me about your divorce?"

Andrea nodded, speechless in how well he put it all into words.

"When you mentioned doing whatever you could to save your marriage," Devon said, staring into her eyes. "That spoke to me. Like, that told me the kind of woman you truly are."

She didn't know what to say to that. She would rather play it off as just an ordinary thing she'd heard before, but with Devon, it was different. It wasn't just lip service. It was coming from his heart. She hadn't lied when she said he wore his heart on his sleeve.

"Come on. Let's get these chairs unloaded from the back of my truck and continue this conversation on my porch," Devon said, motioning for her to join him.

Andrea climbed out of the truck, preparing herself for wherever this conversation would lead her.

CHAPTER TWENTY-TWO

Devon spoke from the heart when it came to Andrea. Having feelings for someone wasn't something he took lightly. Even though his brothers would eventually give him flack for falling first, he would grin and bear it. Because no matter what, he was the one who had to live with himself and the choices he made. If he waited to tell Andrea that she'd taken him by surprise, there was a chance she would be long gone by then. Who knew what she had planned once the wedding was over?

Once he placed the rocking chairs where he wanted them, he patted the empty chair next to him and gestured for Andrea to sit down. She had seemed a little taken aback by what he had said, and he hoped he hadn't caused her to regret spending time with him.

"I have to admit," he started, looking out in the distance and taking in the view surrounding his cabin. He'd taken a lot of things for granted, but he no longer felt the need to do that. He had always been the obnoxious one among his brothers, never wanting to fully embrace maturity, but at the end of the day, that had all been for show. It was a mask to hide how he truly felt. "You aren't who I was expecting when I first saw you."

Andrea laughed but immediately repressed it with a nervous look. "Is that a good thing?"

Devon folded his hands in his lap, fumbling now for the words he needed to tell her what he meant. He tipped his cowboy hat and grunted. "Well, it depends on how you're going to take it."

Andrea leaned back in her chair with wide eyes. "I'm not sure I want to know."

Devon shrugged. "It isn't all that bad, I guess. It's just I was expecting some barrel-racing diva to start barking orders around here, demanding everything be pristine and high-class."

Andrea let out a laugh. If she had been taking a drink, he imagined this was the time she would have spit it out. "Are you kidding?"

Devon bobbed his head side to side. "Maybe."

"And you were wrong in your assumptions?"

"You already know that I was," Devon said with a nervous laugh. "And I hate to admit when I'm wrong, just so you know."

"Of course." Andrea playfully rolled her eyes. "Show me a man who doesn't."

Devon furrowed his brow at her. "Hey, now."

A laugh escaped her lips, and he seemed to enjoy it a little too much. Seeing her laugh after hearing about her past was something he could get used to.

"You took me by surprise, though, I'll give you that," Devon admitted, keeping his eyes locked on hers. "Then you went and offered me dancing lessons. I was a goner right then and there."

"Get out of here," Andrea said, shooing a hand at him. "There's nothing special in offering to teach someone to dance. I just figured if you needed the help, I had the time to teach you."

"You're right, but you haven't seen what you got yourself into," Devon admitted, keeping a smile on his face. "Are you sure the offer's still on the table? If so, why don't you show me a thing or two while we both have time to kill?"

Andrea looked down at his extended hand. "You want me to teach you right now?"

Devon kept his hand out, willing her to take it. "Why not? Are you backing out of your offer?"

Andrea tipped her head back and laughed. She slid further back into the chair and tucked a strand of loose hair behind her ear. She was the most attractive woman when she did subtle things like that, and it sent his heart into a frenzy while waiting for her to take his hand.

"I don't back down from a challenge, cowboy," she said with a confident smile before taking hold of his hand and pulling him out of his chair. "I'll just be thanking the good Lord I'm not wearing a dress."

Devon followed her lead, positioning himself in the front yard and making sure they had enough room to dance without tripping over anything. The last thing he wanted was for them to fall hard on the ground, or worse yet, land in the firepit he planned to use later that night.

He quickly sent a prayer to the man upstairs, praying for the good Lord to help him if he managed to misstep and ended up taking her down with him. Not to mention there was a high probability she would have to encounter him stepping on her feet.

At least if anything horrible did happen, or he made a fool out of himself, he had warned her beforehand. He had told her that he needed all the help he could get, and he hadn't been lying. He just hoped and prayed like crazy he could stay on his feet without causing too much harm.

He would do his best to keep his focus, knowing full well that it would be a difficult task. He was taking lessons from a woman who caused his heart to thrum out of his chest. Maybe he had too much confidence when it came to his ability to focus. Would he even be able to think straight while he held her close?

"Are you sure you're up for this?" Devon was letting his nerves get the best of him.

Andrea looked up at him, still hanging onto his hand. "I've never been so sure about anything in my entire life."

CHAPTER TWENTY-THREE

Unsure what she was truly getting herself into, Andrea reminded herself to let go and just have fun with it. She wouldn't judge Devon too harshly if he didn't get the motions down on the first try.

"Just follow my lead," Andrea said, slowly leading Devon into a dance rhythm until she felt confident he was getting the hang of it.

After a few minutes, it was clear that he wasn't all that bad. At least, not as horrible as he claimed to be at dancing. She ignored the inadequate beating of her heart as she stepped closer to him, closing the distance between them. Devon's hand rested on her lower back, causing her to feel a pang of something she hadn't felt in quite a while. She could count on one hand the number of times she had danced with her ex-husband, and most of those were due to her dragging him to the dance floor at local events.

She shook the thought of her ex-husband from her mind. She didn't want to think about him. Not when she was enjoying this moment with Devon.

"How am I doing?" Devon whispered into her ear as she pressed closer to his chest. She hardly noticed that he was waiting to hear her thoughts as she lost herself in his arms, trying to imagine what life would be like if she decided to stay in Pine Creek.

He shifted, nearly losing his footing, and stepped back from Andrea. He tipped his cowboy hat and studied her. "Am I doing that bad?"

"No, not at all." She glanced up at him. "Are you sure you weren't just saying you were horrible at dancing to get out of it at the reception?"

"Maybe." Devon's cheeks flushed, and she knew she'd caught him red-handed. His broad shoulders shrugged before he spun Andrea around underneath his arm. "It's easier just to let people believe what they want to believe when it comes to certain things."

Andrea paused mid-spin. "Like what?"

Devon dropped her hand, immediately making her wish he hadn't. She wasn't ready for this to end. She had no choice but to follow him back to the porch. So much for enjoying the moment.

He slid into a chair and rocked back and forth while he waited for Andrea to join him. She had to admit the rocking chairs were wonderful, and after dancing for the last several minutes, she decided not to argue about sitting down.

"I'm not sure what all you might've heard about me," Devon said in a soft tone. "Especially from Kate. Much like a few others, she didn't care too much for me when she first met me. Might have had something to do with how obnoxious I was about her dating Beckett at the time…"

His words trailed off as Andrea studied him. He seemed lost in thought, trying to find a way to express himself more clearly for her to understand. But she understood him. In a way, she didn't need to hear the words to know exactly how he felt. She'd lived her whole life trying to make everyone like her. To fit in. If only she knew then what she did now, she would have lived a little more carefree and without fear of what others thought of her.

"That's normal, though, isn't it? Sibling rivalry and all that?" She only asked because she was an only child. She didn't have siblings to joke around with or take jabs at, and she imagined if she did, she might have experienced life a bit differently. "And for the record, Kate might've mentioned it a time or two, but I don't think she meant it in a bad way. She was just giving me a heads up on the dynamics around here."

"There's definitely a lot of that here." Devon glanced at her, seeming to accept Andrea's word for it. He didn't have anything to fear when it came to his family. From what Andrea could tell, they all rallied around one another, stepped up when it was required, and they certainly loved hard. At the end of the day, that's what family was all about. At least, that's what she believed. "I guess what I'm trying to get at, is that it seems there's a lot of expectations, and when I feel like I'm not measuring up, I make up for it by clowning around. But it's all for show because I'm not really that immature. Or at least, I'd like to think I'm not."

Andrea sat quietly, listening to what he had to say. She couldn't imagine growing up with brothers who had everything going for them in life, only to feel like the odd one out. She heard Devon loud and clear, and seeing Devon's true colors, she had to disagree with what Kate told her.

"I think we all feel that way sometimes," Andrea stated matter-of-factly. "I remember a few times in my life that I pretended to be something I wasn't.

Mostly when I was married and trying to juggle everything while working on advancing my career. Everyone thought I was happy and had it all figured out. Boy, were they wrong."

The admission made Andrea sad, but it was the truth. She wanted Devon to know more about her. More than she was willing to share with anyone else. And she wanted to know him better as well.

"Everyone expects so much," Devon said with a shrug. "It's hard to let everyone down… and easier to crack jokes without telling anyone how you truly feel. Especially my parents. After seeing my older brothers, and now my twin, finding love, working hard, and settling down, I hate to know what they think about me. Like I'm slacking or something."

Andrea knew better than to believe that. Porter and Diane seemed to accept things fairly well around the ranch. Even if Diane wanted all six of her boys to find love, get married, and have a family, Andrea couldn't see her turning them away, or loving them any less, if that didn't happen.

But she understood Devon's fear. Not because of her mother, who'd loved her unconditionally, but because of her father and, of course, her ex-husband. They clearly couldn't accept her for who she was, or what she wanted in life. Instead of compromising, they pushed her away and left her fending for herself.

She looked at Devon, still lost in thought. Would he be the type to push her away when things didn't go the way he planned? She couldn't imagine it.

Devon glanced at the watch on his wrist and stood up. "I suppose we should probably head to the main house, so we don't miss supper."

How was it already suppertime? Clearly, Andrea had lost track of time while spending the afternoon with Devon. Not that she minded losing track of time, but she knew how upset Diane would be if she skipped out on another meal at the house.

Andrea stood from the rocking chair and followed him off of the front porch. He reached back for her hand, and she happily accepted it, realizing that maybe letting go and living a more carefree life might be what she needed after all.

CHAPTER TWENTY-FOUR

Devon held Andrea's hand as they walked up the front porch at the main house. Did he want to hold Andrea's hand in front of his family? Of course. He wanted to hold her hand any chance he was given.

What he didn't want was for his brothers to make it awkward. Even though he was the one who made things awkward for them over the last several years, Devon wasn't ready for payback. There was no doubt in his mind that his brothers would give him flack. He just hoped they wouldn't do so in front of Andrea.

But then again, other than his twin brother, Andrea seemed to understand him better than anyone else. Which said a lot considering he'd fallen hard and fast for her. Heck, he didn't even realize they were toeing the line of something more happening between them, and now he was holding her hand and thinking about what the future held.

He shook his head, clearing his thoughts of the future. He didn't need to get carried away. Especially when he didn't even know whether Andrea planned to stick around once the wedding was over.

Would she stay at the ranch? Or would she move on to something better?

"Well, look who finally showed up," his father said, standing from his chair and greeting Andrea with a side hug. He slapped Devon on the shoulder and sat back down. "We were starting to think you didn't like us."

Devon exchanged a look with Andrea before leading her around the dining room table. He picked a spot next to Adam and Mya and pulled out a chair for Andrea to sit in. He slid in next to Adam, who nudged him in the arm and gave him a knowing look.

"Beckett and Kate should be coming any minute, but I'll go ahead and get the food on the table," his mother said, setting a warm casserole dish in the center of the table. "It's going to be good seeing Kate out and about on the ranch. I'm glad she's feeling a lot better."

"Rest was good for her," his father chimed in at

the other end of the table. "She shouldn't have taken on so much."

"Well, I'm just glad that Andrea arrived when she did," his mother admitted, smiling warmly at Andrea from across the table. "The good Lord knows what a blessing you are."

Devon squeezed Andrea's hand underneath the table and smiled at her. She accepted his mother's praise and quietly thanked her.

The back door opened, and footsteps echoed against the hardwood floors of the kitchen as Beckett and Kate rounded the corner of the dining room. Devon greeted Beckett with a quick nod before scooting his chair closer to Adam, making room for his brother and soon-to-be sister-in-law to squeeze in next to them.

He watched as Kate embraced Andrea in a hug before taking the chair Beckett had pulled out for her. Kate waved at everyone, seeming happy to be out of her house and back on her feet. Devon had a feeling she would no longer have to adhere to the doctor's orders to rest now that she appeared to be feeling better.

"How are the wedding plans going?" his father asked before his mother had a chance to call for their evening prayer. His father quickly apologized for interrupting and let them know they would start prayer in a minute. "It seems to me that things are moving right along. The big day will be here before we know it."

Andrea shifted in her chair beside Devon. She exchanged a smile with Kate as Devon waited to hear an update along with the others.

"The dresses will arrive soon, and the tuxes, too," Kate said, glancing around the table at everyone. "We won't have much time to get things altered, so everyone will need to try everything on the day it arrives. Other than that, I think my bridesmaids are doing a great job getting everything lined up and ready to go."

His parents seemed pleased to hear that.

Despite his mother's urgency to say the prayer, she asked Kate, "And the two of you have your honeymoon booked?"

"Hopefully you're not planning to go very far," Devon said with a laugh. All eyes turned to him like he'd opened a can of worms. Thankfully, Kate saved him from the onslaught by telling them there was nothing to worry about.

"We've already booked our stay in a nearby resort," she said, smiling happily at Beckett. "It's not too far away just in case this little girl decides to come early."

"We've talked to the doctor, too. She'll be on call in case Kate goes into labor," Beckett acknowledged. "But we're not expecting that to happen. The doctor assured us that even though Kate hit a rough patch with dehydration and exhaustion, everything else should be smooth sailing. Our little girl will be here on time and not a moment too soon."

Everyone seemed pleased to hear the good news during the quick update from Beckett and Kate. It had only been a couple of weeks since her dizzy spell sent her to the emergency room, but in that time, Devon's family had gotten restless waiting for everything to go back to normal.

"Should we say the prayer now?" his mother suggested, holding her hands out next to her. Devon was already holding Andrea's hand but lifted their interlocked hands onto the table as he took hold of Adam's. The look Adam gave him didn't go unnoticed. There was no doubt that Adam knew the two of them had been holding hands long before the prayer.

Once they prayed, the family ate in silence until his father looked up from his plate and asked Devon, "When are you planning to start working on that old barn up north of the property?"

"I didn't know he was planning to," Hunter, who

was sitting next to Alyssa, chimed in. Devon looked over at Hunter and furrowed a brow. Of course, his brother knew all about the upheaval, but now wasn't the time to bring it up.

"I am," Devon said. He turned and looked at Andrea then back to the rest of his family. "We're actually going to get started on it later today or early tomorrow morning before it gets too hot out."

"We are?" Andrea asked quietly beside him, but not quite low enough for his family not to hear. Devon swallowed a lump in his throat, wondering if he'd made a mistake in assuming she would be willing to help him.

"Well," he said, shifting in his chair and releasing her hand from his. "I just figured since you're in charge of making sure everything gets done…"

His words trailed off when he realized that he might have made a mistake in assuming she'd be okay with helping. He could blame it on wishful thinking. On wanting to spend more time with her. But if she didn't want to, then that was fine, too.

"Uh oh. Trouble in paradise already?" Adam muttered beside him. Devon nudged him in the side and shot him a glare.

It was just a simple misunderstanding. He should have known better than to assume anything when it came to Andrea. Maybe he'd been wrong in thinking she would enjoy helping him reconstruct the barn while telling him how she and Kate planned for it to look in time for the wedding.

Andrea shifted nervously beside him. *Does she not like the idea of helping me?* The two of them would make a great team, and they would have the barn completed in no time. Or at least, that's what he thought anyway.

"I just have so many other things I need to do," Andrea said, looking from Devon to the others sitting around the table. "I don't mind helping with the barn. I'll just need to find the time between trail rides and everything else."

Well, at least she didn't mind the idea. Devon was still kicking himself for not asking her when they were alone. It was foolish to say something in front of his family and put her on the spot.

"I'm sure we can figure it all out," Mya chimed in on the other side of Adam, offering an assuring smile. "Trail rides happen first thing in the mornings, and I don't mind cleaning the cabins. I can work with Kate to get flowers and everything else lined up. We can work together when you're not busy with Devon."

What should have comforted Andrea seemed to do the exact opposite. Devon would wait until they left the main house to talk things over with Andrea. He would reassure her that she didn't need to worry about the barn if she didn't want to.

But for now, he was going to fill up on supper so he could get more work done around the ranch without his stomach protesting in hunger.

CHAPTER TWENTY-FIVE

Andrea felt uncomfortable with the thought of Mya helping Kate with everything wedding related. The whole reason for Andrea being at the ranch was to help Kate—her best friend.

"Hey," Devon called out to her as she left the main house and started walking off in the direction of her cabin. "Wait up."

If she stopped and waited for him to catch up, what would she say to him? That she didn't want to work on the barn with him, even though she really didn't mind. Other than the fact she didn't know a thing about restoring old barns, she wouldn't mind working with Devon and spending more time with him. But that wasn't why she was there.

She wasn't there to fall in love with the best man. She was there to help her best friend with the wedding. And now it felt like she was just there to do the mucky chores and take care of everything other than the wedding. Not to mention taking a backseat to Mya as Kate's best friend. It seemed Mya was eager to step up and take Andrea's place.

Shoving that thought out of her mind, knowing how ridiculous it was, Andrea stopped and waited for Devon to catch up to her. He gently reached for her arm and turned her to face him. She couldn't wipe the angry tears away quickly enough. No sooner had she turned to face him than a look of concern etched was on his handsome face.

"What's going on? Talk to me," Devon demanded, furrowing his brow and impatiently waiting for her to say something. He stared into her eyes, making her feel more seen than understood. How could she explain how she felt without sounding ridiculous and selfish all in the same breath? She was better than that, wasn't she? "If it's about the barn, you don't have to worry about it. I can handle it on my own. I'm sure I can get Owen or someone else to help with it."

Andrea released a heavy sigh and looked away from him. There was no way she could tell him how she felt. What would he think of her? She was competitive, but she didn't want to compete for Kate's friendship.

It all seemed so silly, like something she would have felt during her high school years—not now. So, why did she feel that way?

"Is it about the barn?" Devon asked again, this time more direct in his tone than before. "Just tell me what's bothering you."

She looked into his eyes, searching for assurance. Something to tell her that he would understand if she just told him. "I shouldn't have come here."

Devon released his hold on her arm and took a step back. He scrubbed a hand over his face before releasing a heavy breath. "What? Why would you say that?"

"Kate has Mya to help with the wedding, and I'm sure the ranch can handle the trail rides just fine without me," Andrea shamelessly admitted. It felt good to get it off her chest. What didn't feel good was taking in the look Devon was giving her.

He swiped his hat off and combed a hand through his hair, looking down at the ground in disbelief. "And here I thought it was because I didn't ask you to work with me on the barn before blurting it out at supper."

Maybe she was right to think how ridiculous she

would sound once she told him how she felt about being at the ranch, taking second place in line for her best friend, and not to mention feeling like a complete failure at everything. All within two weeks' worth of time.

His gaze landed on hers, studying her in silence. If she had gotten back to her cabin without Devon by her side, maybe she could have just written in her journal, and she would be fine. Maybe if she hadn't met online with her therapist during her last session, she would have been fine. Instead, that session had ripped off a Band-Aid and left her feeling all the emotions.

"You honestly regret coming to the ranch?"

Devon's question pulled her from her thoughts of what might have been. She looked up at him, feeling angry about saying anything. "I don't know."

Devon combed a hand through his hair again, appearing at a loss for words, and surprised her when he said, "You think coming to the ranch was a huge mistake, but you don't see how much you've lifted Kate's spirits by being here. How much you've lifted mine. Having you at the ranch has been the greatest thing to happen since I don't know when. Before you came here, Kate was spinning in circles, trying to figure out everything on her own. And Mya? She's just doing what she feels is right. She stepped in like the rest of us do when someone needs us. She's not going to take Kate away from you. Kate loves you like a sister. So much so that she warned me not to even look twice at you."

Andrea's outlook on everything softened. His words resonated deeply with her, yet they left no sign of judgment. Kate was like a sister to her.

"You have no idea how much Kate needs you," Devon said, hooking a finger underneath her chin and raising it for her to look him in the eyes. "I need you."

Andrea denied the second half of his statement the moment he said it. She shook her head, having trouble comprehending what that meant. No man had ever really needed her before. Instead, she was taken for granted, chewed up, and spit out when the next woman came along.

"I have no idea what I'm doing with that barn," Devon admitted with a shrug. "I mean, sure, add a few boards here and there, but as far as decorating it and getting the lights placed correctly? I'm going to need your help."

When Devon released a nervous chuckle, Andrea relaxed. It was apparent now that she had gotten herself into an uproar over nothing. Thankfully, Devon had been the one to point it out to her. What would have happened if it had been Kate or Mya instead? Would she have gotten the same response? She might have lost her new friendship with Mya while damaging her sister-like friendship with Kate.

"So, do you still regret coming here, or can we get to work on the barn?"

Andrea nodded with a half-smile, still not convinced her emotions were settled. She would write about everything later. For now, she needed to focus on the task at hand while trying not to let her thoughts and feelings overwhelm her.

CHAPTER TWENTY-SIX

Devon had no clue if what he said made Andrea feel any better, but he knew that he had told her the truth. Before she arrived at the ranch, he had worked from sunup to sundown, trying to keep his distance from all the mushy stuff around him. At one point, he even considered moving off the ranch to get away from all the talk about the upcoming wedding and avoid the relationships starting all around him.

Thankfully, he had stayed. If he had left the ranch, he wouldn't have met Andrea. And after he got past his original thought of her being a barrel-racing diva, he knew she was someone pretty special.

A part of him hated to admit it, but he would be lying if he said she hadn't knocked him off his feet after just one look. Maybe that's why Kate had told him to behave himself. Did she know there was a chance the two of them would connect as well as they did?

But even then Kate hadn't known about Andrea's divorce. That had to be the reason for her concern, right?

None of that mattered now or at any time during the last few weeks while they worked tirelessly together. Once Andrea agreed to help him with the barn, they began work quickly, and now it was almost finished. All it needed was a fresh coat of paint, and they'd call it good.

He gave her plenty of space when she needed it, and it seemed to work out for both of them. Now, if his brothers would stop giving him flack about falling first, maybe he could focus on getting more work done.

"Who knew that you'd be falling in love so soon?" Hunter asked, jabbing Devon with an elbow.

"Especially since you're the one always giving us heck about it," Adam chided, looking at Beckett for backup in their conversation. "Now look at you."

"Cut it out," Devon said, tossing a warning look at his brothers. "I'm going to run into town and pick up some paint. When I get back, you better be ready to chip in and help."

Adam and Hunter took a step back, throwing their hands up and shaking their heads. Beckett smirked with a shrug and offered to help once he finished baling more hay. They had a good number of square bales stacked up near the old barn, but Devon supposed a few more wouldn't hurt considering they weren't sure on the number of guests to expect at the wedding. They wanted to have plenty of seating for everyone.

"I thought Andrea was on board to help you finish that project," Hunter said, raising a brow. "What'd you do? Scare her off?"

"She went into town with Kate and Mya to pick up the dresses. She said something about tasting a few different flavors of cupcakes from Mrs. Langley before heading back to the ranch." Devon still couldn't believe the wedding was less than two weeks away. Time seemed to fly now that they had spent so much time restoring the barn and getting everything else in line. "I'm sure they won't be back for a few more hours, and I'd like to get most of the barn painted before dark."

He didn't dare mention what his intentions were once the sun went down. He would never hear the end of it. They already gave him plenty of unsolicited advice when it came to Andrea. Did they honestly think Devon was willing to risk messing anything up with her?

On that note, he decided to leave his brothers and move along. He needed to head into town and grab the paint soon if he had any hope of surprising Andrea.

What he hadn't planned on was running into Ruby at the hardware store. Of course, she talked about all things wedding related, but she also managed to ask if the rumors were true about Devon and Andrea. He wasn't one to lie, and he certainly wouldn't deny his feelings when it came to Andrea.

"You've heard right," Devon admitted with a smile. He placed the gallons of paint in the back of his truck while Ruby leaned against the tailgate. "It's good to know that the old rumor mill's still up and running."

He closed the tailgate with a quick laugh as Ruby stepped away from the truck. She followed him to the driver's side door and leaned against the metal frame, resting her arms along the window tracks. "You know I have quite an assortment of engagement rings. I have no doubt you'll find the perfect one if you want to stop in sometime."

Devon smiled, appreciating Ruby's offer. "Maybe sometime, but I don't think that's going to be soon. I'm taking it one day at a time and seeing what happens. I've never been one to rush things."

"I know that. I'm just saying. You know where to look when you're ready." Ruby patted the truck's door and smiled. "Tell your mother hello from me, and I'll see everyone at the wedding."

Devon nodded as he shifted the old truck into reverse and backed out of the parking spot in front of the hardware store. Leave it to Ruby to make him think about when the perfect time to propose would be. Not that he hadn't thought about it. He'd spent a lot of nights lately wondering what the future held for them.

But like he told Ruby, he wasn't one to rush things. He would know when the time was right, but until then, he planned to take it one day at a time. First, he needed to get back to the ranch and get that darned barn painted.

If everything went as planned tonight, Devon would have a good idea about where their relationship was headed and what he had to look forward to.

CHAPTER TWENTY-SEVEN

The past three weeks were a blur for Andrea, and she still couldn't believe they were down to the last two weeks before the wedding. The big day was right around the corner, and as luck would have it, the dresses fit. She silently thanked God for the answered prayer, knowing they were short on time and alterations wouldn't have been completed in time.

With Devon putting the finishing touches on the barn, Andrea had gone along with Kate and Mya to not only pick up the dresses, but also swing by Charlotte Langley's for a plate of cupcakes.

Charlotte greeted them at the door of her small house, warmly inviting them to come inside. Kate introduced Andrea, a smile beaming on her face when

Charlotte wrapped her tiny arms around Andrea and hugged her.

"It's so nice to meet you," Charlotte said, patting Andrea's cheek like a grandmother would their grandchild. "I've heard nothing but great things about you, and I'm certain you'll find what you're looking for here in Pine Creek… *if* you haven't already found it."

The older woman winked at Andrea as she took a step back, motioning for them to follow her into the dining room where a display of cupcakes awaited them. Andrea glanced at Kate, unsure what all Kate had mentioned to Charlotte. Why would the woman insist she would find what she was looking for? She didn't even know what she was looking for, and she knew herself a lot better than the woman who just met her did.

Kate must have picked up on Andrea's apprehension, because she rested a hand on her arm and smiled. "She means well. Small towns know everything about everyone."

Andrea settled her thoughts. If she was going to stay in Pine Creek, she might as well get used to how things spread like wildfire. Aside from the slight unease she felt from the woman's words, she found a sense of peace within them as well. Maybe she had found exactly what she was looking for without even looking.

"I have plenty of flavors for you girls to try," Charlotte said, pointing to the assortment on the table. "Go ahead and take whatever you want. Just be sure to let me know which flavor you decide on for the wedding soon, so I can make sure to have them baked and ready for you."

Charlotte handed each of them an empty paper plate and smiled. "My favorite is the red velvet, but I know that's not a favorite to many."

Kate smiled with a nod as she grabbed the various cupcakes and divided them up on each plate. Even though Andrea had worked up an appetite, she wasn't sure she could handle eating this many cupcakes—at least not all in one day. She had a sweet tooth, and she couldn't deny that just the sight of the heavily frosted cupcakes made her mouth water in anticipation.

Once they each had a plateful of cupcakes, they told Charlotte how much they appreciated her and promised to let her know their decision soon.

Next stop was the restaurant. *Pine's Wine and Dine* was nestled along the highway on the outskirts of town. If someone drove through town and blinked, they would miss it.

Over the last couple of days, the three of them had

ventured into the restaurant and tried a few selections on the menu. Each divided their meals and provided feedback amongst themselves on what they liked the most. It didn't take them long to decide which three-course meal would be served at the reception.

Today, they needed to confirm exactly what they wanted and schedule catering times with the restaurant, which took less than ten minutes to accomplish before they were walking back to the truck and heading to the ranch.

"I can't believe how smoothly everything's going," Kate announced happily. The smile on her face told Andrea just how pleased her friend was with their planning success. "I still can't believe I'm getting married in less than two weeks."

Andrea agreed wholeheartedly, knowing it was exactly what her best friend deserved. No matter how her own marriage had ended, she refused to believe the same would happen for Kate. Beckett was a true gentleman. It hadn't taken long for Andrea to realize that Kate had found the man of her dreams. A man who put everything and everyone before himself, making sure his bride-to-be had not only what she wanted, but what she needed.

Despite the ongoing conversation happening around her, Andrea's mind filled with thoughts on what the future might hold for her. If she decided to stay in Pine Creek, would she find happiness? Would her own dreams come true?

She thought about her budding relationship with Devon. Was God giving her a chance at finding her own happily ever after? Could it be as simple as falling for Devon?

They pulled off of the highway and turned into the ranch's entrance. Andrea took in the sight around her, taking in the beautiful backdrop the mountains in the distance provided, as well as the wide-open space surrounding the property. Pleasantly lined with cabins and evergreen trees, it provided a welcoming sense of home. Perhaps Charlotte had been right in suggesting she'd found what she was looking for even if she hadn't been actively searching for it, nor did she know what she could possibly need the most.

Kate parked the truck in a vacant spot near the main house and turned to face Andrea and Mya. "I can't thank you guys enough for everything you've done and continue to do. I couldn't have done all of this alone, and for that, I'm forever thankful for you both."

Tears welled in Kate's eyes as she fanned her face. "Ugh, these hormones. I told myself I wasn't going to cry."

Andrea and Mya shared a laugh and hugged Kate. Once they'd hugged it out, Mya reached for the cupcakes they'd received from Charlotte and said, "Let's get these inside before they melt."

She climbed out of the truck, handing a plate to Andrea with a smile. "I'm sure Diane will want to try some, too. I think it's safe to say we won't be able to eat all of these without a little help deciding."

Kate and Andrea exchanged an agreeable nod as the three of them walked up the porch steps and signaled their arrival as they entered the house.

"Oh, how lovely," Diane announced, motioning for them to place the cupcakes on the kitchen counter. "Charlotte never fails to amaze me. What all do we have here?"

Kate busied herself pointing out the different flavors on each plate as footsteps on the porch tore Andrea's focus toward the door. She didn't see Devon before leaving the ranch with Kate and Mya, and for a split second, she wondered if it could be him walking into the main house.

She knew the chance of that was slim. He was most likely busy painting the barn, which caused a pang of guilt. She should be out there helping him instead of tasting cupcakes.

The door opened, and she caught a glimpse of

who was walking into the house. *This must be the brother who's been out of town.* The man waltzed into the kitchen with a beautiful woman trailing behind him. She smiled and waved at Andrea, introducing herself as Lacy before turning to her other half and introducing him as well. "The one who's taking stock of the cupcakes is William."

Andrea laughed as the man grabbed two cupcakes—one for him and one for Lacy.

"You must be Andrea." William stopped next to her and extended his free hand. "I've heard a lot of good things about you. I hear you're keeping Devon in line around here."

Andrea laughed at that. She wouldn't go as far as saying she was keeping him in line, but she would agree that she'd given him plenty of things to do around the ranch to prepare for the wedding.

"Hopefully he's been good to you," William said, popping the remaining bite of cupcake into his mouth and wiping his hand on his jeans. "If not, I'll make sure and have a talk with him."

Before Andrea could defend Devon, Mya took it upon herself to mention the one thing Andrea was hesitant on sharing with his brother. "You haven't heard? Devon fell head over boots for Andrea. He was smitten the moment he met her."

Andrea mouthed the word "thanks" to Mya, praying William wouldn't say too much about it. Even though, from what she could tell, he seemed pleased with the idea. "About time."

Kate offered a cupcake to Andrea. "Try this one. I think it might be the winner."

Andrea hesitated before accepting the cupcake. Her nerves had gotten the best of her once Mya mentioned how suddenly Devon had fallen for her.

She took a small bite, savoring the tastes of vanilla and champagne buttercream frosting. The flavors melted in her mouth, and she immediately settled on this being the one they had to choose.

"She also has vanilla with salted caramel drizzled over the frosting, but I think I like the one you have the best," Kate said, taking one matching Andrea's from the plate and biting into it. "Nothing says 'wedding' like the perfect blend of vanilla and champagne."

"That settles that," Mya said with a confident smile. "Do you want me to tell Charlotte?"

Once they agreed on a set amount for the woman to bake, Andrea and Kate agreed that Mya would call Charlotte and let her know.

William and Lacy grabbed the last two cupcakes on their way out of the house. "We hate to eat and run, but after spending the last several hours on the road, I'm ready for a shower."

"Well, wait a minute," Diane said, stopping them both from leaving too soon. "Tell me how everyone's doing. You get your parents all taken care of?"

Diane focused on Lacy, and though Andrea had no idea what they were talking about, she hoped Lacy's parents were okay.

"Yes, they're fine. They were glad to have us there to help after the tornado went through," Lacy said, glancing over at William. "William helped my brothers get some things repaired, like the barn and a few of the smaller cabins while I watched my niece and helped my mom with things at the house."

"They still need a lot of work done around there, but we mentioned heading back that way once the wedding was over," William said, nodding toward Kate. "We didn't want to miss it."

Andrea could only imagine what Lacy's family went through while she talked about the tornado. Andrea had been lucky not to see one firsthand while living in Texas, and she was thankful Lacy's family had survived the catastrophe.

Willliam and Lacy gave one final goodbye, letting Andrea know it was a pleasure to finally meet her.

They promised to see everyone early in the morning for breakfast.

Mya offered to help Diane clean up the kitchen while Kate cleared the plates from the counter and threw them away. Andrea thought about what she could do next, and figured now was the time to duck out and see if there was anything she could help Devon with.

CHAPTER TWENTY-EIGHT

Devon had just finished placing a second coat of paint on the old barn doors and made it to the horse barn when he caught a glimpse of Andrea's truck heading toward the horse barn—probably to check on Stella.

Of course, that couldn't happen until nightfall, so he needed to think on his feet and distract her with something else. Maybe she would agree to go on the trails with him and Buck once he got cleaned up. Right now, he was covered head to toe in splatters of red paint and sweat—a clear indication he shouldn't think twice about taking a shower, given the opportunity.

"Hey, cowboy," Andrea called out as she climbed out of her truck and made her way over to where he was standing. From a distance, she could see the barn, which he didn't mind. It was what awaited her inside that he didn't want her to see just yet. Not until the time was right.

"Hey," he said, running a hand through his sweat-matted hair. "I thought you'd still be with Kate and Mya."

Andrea smiled and shook her head. She hooked a thumb over her shoulder and said, "No, they're helping Diane clean up the house in time for supper. I figured I'd come find you and see if there was anything you need me to do."

Devon glanced over his shoulder at the freshly painted barn and looked back at Andrea. "I think I've got everything taken care of here. I was actually thinking about hitting the trails with Buck."

He wrapped an arm around her middle and pulled her close to him. Despite being covered in paint, she didn't seem to mind. She smiled at him when a splotch of paint transferred from his overalls to her shirt. "Sorry about that," he said, offering a slight grin. "If you want to join me on the trails, I'll get cleaned up."

"You're not tired after working on the barn all day?"

"I'll never be too tired to ride my horse," he said

with a mindless shrug. "Besides, if it means spending more time with you, I'm all for it. We have, what? A good hour or two before it gets dark?"

He wouldn't mention what his plans were for after dark. He would patiently wait for the sun to set and the hours to tick by once they finished eating supper with the family. Hunter had helped him set up the barn for his reveal, and even Owen surprised him by offering to help as well. Owen wasn't too happy with Devon or Andrea because they'd emptied the metal building where the Christmas displays were kept.

Devon listened to Owen vent the entire time he helped. He wasn't looking forward to setting everything back up in time for Christmas, and it didn't seem to matter much when Devon told him they still had a while before they needed to worry about it. He knew his brother didn't care for the holiday, much less setting up the metal building with the displays. To him, it felt like torture. To Devon, it seemed like a way to get Owen to lend a hand in hopes that it would change the way he felt while spreading some Christmas cheer.

Thankfully, there would still be plenty of time for all of that after the wedding. Right now, Devon wanted to focus on something more important, like getting Andrea to go on a trail ride with him so she wouldn't focus on the barn.

"What do you say?" Devon asked. As he leaned in, closing the distance between them, his gaze focused on her lips. He swiped his thumb along the side of her mouth, clearing the evidence leftover from eating cupcakes. "You missed some frosting."

Andrea's eyes met his and, at that moment, he wanted nothing more than to kiss her. Heck, he'd wanted to kiss her the day they danced at his cabin, but the timing hadn't felt right. But now, while staring into her eyes, there was no doubt in his mind about whether the timing was right.

He swept a strand of her hair from the side of her face, gently tucking it behind her ear as he leaned in. His lips brushed gently against hers, and he relaxed as she leaned into his kiss. He had never wanted something as much as he needed this. It was the moment he had been waiting for to let him know that he hadn't made a mistake in falling for her. There was a chance she wanted this as much as he did.

The moment was abruptly interrupted by a shout in the distance. He pulled away from Andrea, mumbling under his breath as he looked at the person responsible for breaking them apart. Hunter waved a hand over his head as he rode toward them, saddled on Ryker's back.

"I thought you two would want to be there when Pops gives Kate her gift," Hunter said, ignoring the fact that he'd interrupted something good. Frustrated, Devon combed a hand through his hair. "But I understand if you have better things to do."

Andrea looked from Hunter to Devon. Devon couldn't be too upset. He'd been waiting just as long as everyone else to see Kate's face light up when their father presented her with his masterpiece.

"Hold that thought," he whispered to Andrea before agreeing to meet with the rest of the family at the woodshop. Andrea smiled as she climbed into the passenger seat of her truck and Devon took hold of the steering wheel.

He glanced over at her on the way to the woodshop. She seemed to be lost in her own thoughts, and he prayed she wasn't having second thoughts about what just happened between them.

CHAPTER TWENTY-NINE

Kissing Devon distracted her from wanting to see the rest of the barn, but she hadn't expected the moment to be interrupted by his brother. Kate had been right when she told her there was never a dull moment on the ranch.

As they arrived at the woodshop, Andrea thought about the crib Porter had made for Kate. For the family's first-born grandchild. A familiar emotion jolted through Andrea as she thought about the times she'd spent searching for the perfect crib. She'd set up the entire nursery in two days, just to have her dream shattered by a ruthless nightmare.

She was happy for Kate, but that happiness didn't

comfort the ache she felt from missing out on the chance of being a mother herself.

Devon's lingering gaze caught her attention, pulling her from her thoughts. Thankfully, no tears had been shed. She would have a hard time explaining them to Devon, especially when they were wrapped in a memorable moment.

Kate was the last to arrive, led into the shop by Beckett. They even went as far as placing a blindfold over her eyes to keep her guessing about where they had brought her.

Everyone crowded into the woodshop, surrounding Porter who stood proudly beside the sheet-covered crib, counting down the minutes for the big reveal.

"Katie Cat," Porter said, his voice soft as she approached him, following Beckett's lead. Porter reached out and took hold of her hand, gently squeezing it as he appeared to gather his thoughts. "Diane and I have been waiting for this moment, and I can't tell you how difficult it was not to bring something with us to the baby shower."

Kate let out a light cry, covering her mouth with her hand. Andrea approached Kate's side and rested a hand on her arm, letting her know she was there.

"But I couldn't give you something that wasn't

quite ready," Porter said with a light chuckle. "I wanted to make sure it was perfect for that little girl of yours."

On Porter's cue, Beckett removed the blindfold at the same time Porter pulled back the sheet on the crib. He smiled proudly with tears glistening in his eyes as he presented Kate with a gift, not only of love but of hard work and dedication.

Kate brought her hands to her face, tears streaming down her cheeks. Andrea hugged Kate, knowing how much this meant to her. There were a few times Andrea had almost let it slip about the crib shortly after seeing it. One of those times happened recently when Kate showed her the nursery she'd prepared for her baby girl. She'd mentioned being unable to find the perfect crib, and Andrea had bitten her tongue from telling her all about the one Porter had made for her.

"I don't know what to say." Kate stammered over her words, obviously experiencing a mix of emotions and having a hard time finding the right words to explain how she felt. Andrea understood completely.

Porter and Diane wrapped their arms around Kate, and Andrea took a step back, giving them space to enjoy the moment together.

A strong arm wrapped around her waist. "I hope

those are tears of happiness," Devon whispered, his breath warm against her ear.

She nodded, though she hadn't realized tears were streaming down her cheeks. She quickly wiped them away with the back of her hand and did her best to keep her composure as relentless memories of her past flooded her mind.

"Hey," Devon whispered, nudging her slightly. "Everything okay?"

Andrea felt her heart breaking no matter how hard she fought to keep it together. This wasn't about her, and though she was happy for Kate, she couldn't stop thinking about the life she once had. About the baby she almost had.

Devon led her from the woodshop, refusing to leave her side once they were outside. Andrea inhaled the fresh air, relieved from the feeling of suffocation while the tears continued streaming down her cheeks despite her best efforts to make them stop.

She didn't want to cause a scene. She wanted to be there for Kate, but her emotions ricocheted inside of her, battling to be felt and showing no mercy until the feeling of sadness won. Andrea ducked for cover, not wanting anyone to see the mess she was in, including Devon.

But Devon didn't leave her side.

"Andrea, what's wrong? Talk to me," Devon whispered, concern etched in his voice. "Are you okay?"

Andrea shook her head. It was the only answer she could give right now, and though she felt foolish for having broken down like this, she was thankful Devon was there for her. Would he still be standing there when she told him about her past? What the doctors had told her after several miscarriages?

She had seen the look in his eyes as he watched his father unveil the crib. *Has the thought crossed his mind of making a crib for his own child someday? And what will he say when I tell him that I can't give him that? More than that, is our relationship even that serious, or have I let my imagination run away with me?*

"I'm happy for her," Andrea blurted out, feeling embarrassed that fact might not be as obvious to some as it was to her.

"I know that." Devon shifted his weight, still holding her tightly as he lifted her chin and stared into her eyes. "But that's not why you're crying. Something's bothering you, and I want to know what it is."

Andrea inhaled a deep, unsteady breath, then released it slowly. She didn't have time to think about the consequences of telling Devon everything. If she was going to stay in Pine Creek, and if they were going to be together, she needed to be honest with him. She needed to tell him that she might not be the one for him.

"I can't give you those kinds of things," Andrea said. Then she quickly added, "I'm not sure I can give you everything you want in life. I'm broken."

"What?" Devon took a step back but still held onto her. "What are you talking about? This is all about the crib?"

Of course, he was confused. They hadn't even talked about the possibility of a future together. Andrea had jumped the gun, and now, from the looks of it, she took her assumption too far. Maybe she shouldn't have said anything.

"Andrea, listen," Devon said, leading her over to a nearby chair. "I have no idea what you're saying, but I'm willing to try and understand. Just break it down for me, please. Because right now, I have no idea why a crib has anything to do with us."

Andrea looked into his eyes. Concern mixed with confusion in a fierce battle. "If I stay here and we're together," she started, failing to hold back the tears, "I can't give you what Kate has given Beckett. I can't give you children of our own."

Devon sat back and scrubbed a hand over his face.

She couldn't tell what he was thinking or how he took the bombshell she'd just dropped. But she'd needed to tell him before things got more serious than they were. If it was a dealbreaker, she would understand.

"I just want you to know that I'm broken," she said, restating her bottom line. "Before you get too attached, I thought you needed to know. I'm sorry."

She stood, barely able to get her footing as she tried to leave. Devon reached out and grabbed her arm, gently pulling her back toward him. "Wait."

Andrea's heart stopped beating, and she held her breath. This was it. This was the part she was used to. He was going to tell her that maybe their relationship should end, even though it had just begun, and he would send her on her way.

"Life isn't all about getting married and having kids," Devon said, looking intently at her. There was an earnestness in his eyes she had yet to witness from him before, and judging by that alone, he wouldn't let her go without a fight. "I couldn't care less about any of that. Sure, maybe one day I'd like to get married, but that's not what I want to focus on. Marriage isn't the be-all and end-all. Sure, it's something to look forward to, but I can understand if you don't want that. And as far as children…"

His words trailed off as he placed a hand on the

back of his neck. He blew out a heavy breath and shook his head, looking down at the ground. Andrea waited for the ball to drop. He'd said all the right things, but what if not having kids was a dealbreaker? Could she stop her feelings for him and walk away from the life she so easily envisioned living on the ranch with him?

Devon inhaled a deep breath and released it as he leaned back. "I don't even know how to say this without it coming out all wrong."

"I'm sorry," Andrea whispered, regretting having brought it up in the first place. She should have controlled her emotions and prevented them from getting the best of her, especially when she was supposed to be inside sharing the moment with Kate.

"No," Devon said, turning to face her. "You don't have anything to apologize for. That's not at all what I'm saying. I just didn't expect to have this conversation with you. I had no idea that you felt you weren't good enough for me because of everything you've been through. I should be the one apologizing to you."

Andrea wiped the tears from her cheeks and raised a brow. *Why would he be the one to apologize to me?*

"I don't know if I've said anything to make you

think that's all I care about, or made you question your worth," Devon started, reaching out and taking hold of her hand, "but that wasn't my intention at all. All of that talk about my mother wanting me to get married and have kids. That was just me talking. Honestly, I couldn't care less about any of that. As long as I'm happy, and you're happy, being together is all that matters."

"Is everything alright out here?" Beckett rounded the corner, finding both of them in their hiding spot. Beckett looked from Andrea to Devon, apparently noticing the tears streaming down her face. "I was just coming to find you and ask for your help getting this crib back to my place."

Devon stood from his spot next to Andrea. "Yeah, I can do that."

He glanced back at Andrea before looking at his brother. "Everything's fine here. Just give us a few minutes, okay?"

Beckett nodded, taking a second look at Andrea. She could only imagine what he was thinking, but it had nothing to do with Devon. His family seemed to think he wasn't the politest, gentlest man when it came to guests, but they were wrong. He was both of those things and so much more.

"Are we okay? Better yet, are *you* okay?" Devon

asked, kneeling in front of her. "I want to make sure you're not thinking about running out of here the first chance you get."

A soft laugh escaped her lips at his attempt to lighten the mood.

"Yes, I'm fine. We're fine," Andrea whispered. "I should find Kate. She's probably looking for me."

Devon straightened in front of her and helped her from the chair. He wrapped his strong arms around her, pulling her close to him. The embrace was warm and comforting, but the words he whispered in her ear were everything.

"I like you a lot, and I don't care what your ex said or thought about you. You're perfect just the way you are, and your happiness is all that matters to me."

Andrea released her hold on him as he took a step back. He focused his eyes on her. There was no doubt about anything he'd said. She believed him when he'd said it. She had nothing to worry about when it came to finding what she needed at the ranch. She would have all of that and more if she had Devon Carlson by her side.

CHAPTER THIRTY

Andrea's words had hit him like a ton of bricks. He hadn't expected those words to come out of her mouth when he asked her what was wrong. It was obvious now how broken she was from her past, and he hated that man for breaking her. He hated the doctor for telling her she couldn't have kids. Miracles happened every day, and yet, that hadn't stopped the doctor from shattering Andrea's hopes and dreams.

Devon couldn't imagine what Andrea was going through, but he would be the first to tell her that she was worth so much more than a wedding ring and a baby combined. She was a light in his darkness, and he would be damned if he didn't reciprocate that for her.

He hadn't even thought of marriage, or having kids, until she arrived and it slapped him in the face. And though he wanted to find someone to share the rest of his life with, that didn't necessarily mean they had to get married. That's just what society wanted every couple to believe. He knew better than that. He knew several couples around town that were the happiest they'd ever been without tying the knot.

"You sure everything's alright?" Beckett asked, loading the crib into the back of his truck with Devon's help. "I'm not one to pry, but after seeing Andrea in tears—"

"It's fine," Devon said, cutting his brother off.

"Well, if you want to talk about it, I'm here," his brother offered. Beckett latched the crib in place with bungee cords and slammed the tailgate closed. He turned to face Devon, a look of concern etched in his dark features. "From what Kate has told me, Andrea's going through a rough patch. I just want to make sure she's doing okay, and that you're not making it worse."

His brother's last words were delivered with a light, joking tone, and Devon hated to admit there had been a time when it might've been true. But not where Andrea was concerned. Maybe Devon hadn't always been the most pleasant person to be around, with his obnoxious ways and never-ending jabs, but things were different now.

"I'm joking, bro," Beckett said, climbing into the driver's side of his truck and motioning for Devon to hop in. "I know you've been good to her. I knew the minute you kicked into gear to save her from that bear that you cared about her."

Once Devon was in the passenger seat, he thought about everything Andrea had said. He couldn't imagine how she must be feeling while planning a wedding for her best friend, who was also pregnant. He wasn't sure how the woman's mind worked, but he knew there had to be some tug of war happening in Andrea's.

Then he thought about Beckett's words and what seeing her being chased by a bear had done to him. It was no different than how Beckett responded the time Kate had been thrown from the saddle shortly after arriving at the ranch.

"I don't know all the details, nor do I really care to," Beckett admitted, gripping the steering wheel and guiding the truck toward his place, "but I do know that she came to the ranch in search of something. Maybe Kate was right about Andrea needing a break away from the city, but I have a feeling she came here in search of peace. A place to find herself, maybe?"

Devon could see that. It wasn't news to him that she had offered to come to the ranch after going through her divorce. And it wasn't news to him that she needed a chance to find herself. Whether that meant finding peace or something else, Devon was certain she had found it.

"And I think you've helped her with that," Beckett said, shrugging as he turned into the driveway by his place. He shifted the truck into park and looked over at Devon. "I won't say anything more about it because it's not my business, but I feel like maybe things might be moving a little too fast between you two. The best advice I can give you is to slow things down a notch and let her catch her breath."

Devon grunted. Advice coming from his brother who let Kate walk away the first time? Devon was willing to do whatever he needed to in order to give her space, but he didn't think he was crowding her.

"Let's get this crib unloaded, so I can get back to baling hay," Beckett said, climbing out of the truck and glancing back at Devon.

Devon unloaded the crib with his brother and helped carry it into the cabin. Once it was placed where Beckett wanted it, Devon thought about his plans for the night.

Does it make sense to carry out my original plan,

or should I just wait? Maybe Beckett was right. Maybe he needed to take a step back and give her some breathing room.

Conflicted, Devon refused Beckett's offer to give him a ride back to the ranch. A walk would help him clear his mind before he decided what to do next.

CHAPTER THIRTY-ONE

Andrea followed Kate into the main house a short while later, expecting to see Devon sitting at the table. When she didn't see him, she questioned if what she'd told him scared him off. He hadn't seemed too bothered by it. In fact, his words seemed earnest.

So why did it feel like he was now somehow avoiding her? Granted, she had been preoccupied with threading bouquets of wildflowers together while chatting with Kate. Mya had something come up with Adam, so it had been a good time to talk to her best friend alone about her conversation with Devon.

Thankfully, Kate confirmed what Devon had told

Andrea, which made her feel better. Kate swore up and down that Devon wasn't the type who wanted something just because everyone else had it—including marriage and children. He wasn't willing to settle down with someone just because he was expected to.

Realizing she was thinking too much about it, Andrea made her way to the table and joined the rest of the family for supper. Not seeing Devon at the house surprised her, but maybe something more important needed his attention. Who was to say the cattle hadn't wrecked another fence?

"Who wants to lead the prayer?" Diane asked, glancing around the table. Andrea had a lot to be thankful for, but she didn't feel up to leading it. "Anyone?"

"I will," Lacy offered with a smile.

With hands held around the table, Lacy led them in prayer. Andrea bowed her head and listened intently to Lacy's words. Once she ended the prayer with an "*amen*," the chatter began around the table.

The back door opened and closed followed by heavy footfalls on the hardwood floors. Devon rounded the corner, locking eyes with Andrea as he made his way to the bathroom. "Sorry I'm late. I had to finish one last thing before calling it a night."

To Andrea, he said, "I'm going to wash up, and then I'll join you."

Andrea's heart skipped a beat as she released a slow breath. Her worries about Devon avoiding her had been for nothing. She could relax knowing everything was going to be okay.

It didn't take long before Devon slid in next to her at the table. "Thanks for saving me a spot."

He shot her a wink that sent her heart into overdrive. Despite the fact she hadn't actually saved him a seat, she appreciated him sitting next to her.

"When we're done eating, there's something I want to show you," Devon said. Conversation buzzed around them—talk about the weather, the upcoming auction, and last-minute details for the wedding. But all Andrea could focus on was what Devon had to show her.

She finished eating the rest of the food on her plate and waited patiently for Devon. She didn't mind the wait, but if she were to be honest, she wasn't too good at waiting. Especially knowing there was something he wanted her to see. What could it be?

She had no idea. But thankfully, she was about to find out.

No sooner had Devon finished the last bite of his food than he set his fork down and scrubbed his face with a napkin. He politely excused them from the table, leaving the family to their own endless chatter.

"Don't be so nervous," Devon said, giving her hand a shake. "I can feel how tense you are. Relax. I think you're going to love it."

He shrugged. "Or, at least, I hope so anyway."

Andrea picked up her pace to keep up with him as they made it to the end of the driveway near the main house. His truck was parked behind Beckett's a good distance from the house. She glanced over at the horse barn, a pang of guilt hitting her. She needed to make time for Stella. Other than the trail rides with several groups, she hadn't spent much time with her horse.

"Watch your step," Devon said, holding the passenger side door open for her. She appreciated his chivalry, which was something many women took for granted these days. She wasn't one of them. "Any guesses?"

She could think of a few places Devon could take her, but she crossed off two of the four since they had just finished eating supper. He wouldn't take her to Sunrise Café or Pine's Wine and Dine. That left two other places wide open.

Either he was going to take her back to his place

to test out the rocking chairs he'd made yet again, or he was going to take her to the barn.

She was fine with either, though she really wanted to see the barn. The rocking chairs were nice, but the barn had been calling her name since Devon completed the updates.

"The barn?"

"Ding, ding, ding. We have a winner," Devon announced, ringing an invisible bell above the steering wheel as he guided the truck along the gravel driveway leading them to her best guess. "Winner winner chicken dinner."

"But we just had dinner," she declared with a laugh. If he was this silly on a day-to-day, she was more than okay with that. Maybe his family thought it was obnoxious, but not her. She thought it was a sign of who he truly was. Light-hearted and carefree—something she needed lessons on.

He parked the truck next to the old—but now restored and newly painted—barn and killed the engine. "I would've left the headlights on, but we won't need them. After spending the last two days with grumpy Owen, the barn now has lighting."

Andrea laughed at Devon's reference to Owen. That brother did seem a bit grumpy, but she didn't know him well enough to judge him. Maybe he had a reason for it.

Devon hopped out of the driver's seat and rounded the front of the truck to her side. He opened the door for her and extended a hand in front of him. "And I think you're going to love it."

Andrea carefully stepped out of the truck, cautiously avoiding holes and uneven ground as she walked beside Devon.

It was pretty dark out now that the sun had set behind the mountains, but a slit of soft light shined through the cracks of the old barn. The doors were closed, and to her surprise, they didn't creak when Devon pushed them open.

Andrea felt like she had walked into the barn of her dreams as she took in the sight before her. The brothers had made several floor-to-ceiling repairs, which she admired, but it was a small table—with a perfectly positioned centerpiece full of wildflowers—in the middle of the barn's aisle that fully captured her attention.

A bottle of wine sat in an ice bucket, surrounded by two wine glasses. But not only that, there were two individually wrapped cupcakes at each spot at the small table. Candles glowed in the dim lighting, presenting a truly romantic scene playing out in front of her.

"The cupcakes were a last-minute touch," Devon said, guiding her toward the table. "I didn't want them to melt, or for the horse flies to help themselves to our dessert. I know it's probably not the most roman—"

"It's perfect," Andrea said, interrupting him before he had a chance to complete his sentence. She wouldn't allow him to think for one minute that this wasn't romantic. This was something pulled straight out of the movies. Granted, the cupcakes were an added unique touch, but she was thoroughly impressed.

He closed the doors behind them and pulled a chair back from the table, motioning for her to take a seat. Without hesitation, she sat down and slid the chair closer to the table while he sat down across from her.

"What would you like to start with? The cupcakes or the wine?" The grin pulling at his lips was enough to make her want to skip everything and pick up where they left off before being interrupted by Hunter before the crib reveal.

"Why not both?" Andrea suggested with a slight grin of her own.

Devon pointed at her. "I like your way of thinking."

She watched as he pulled the bottle of wine from the ice bucket and popped the cork. Normally, she would only drink wine on special occasions, but honestly, tonight felt like a special occasion that warranted a glass of wine. Or two.

Devon poured their drinks and offered hers with a wink. If he didn't stop winking like that, he would have another thing coming besides cupcakes and wine.

He sat down in his chair and lifted his glass. She raised her glass to meet his, then smiled. "Cheers to a fresh start and a new beginning. We might not have seen eye to eye at first, but we still managed to make a great team. And I don't know about you, but the heart knows what it wants, and mine wants you. Today, tomorrow, or however long you're willing to put up with me."

Andrea tipped her head back and laughed before tapping her glass with his. The subtle clink of their glasses colliding acknowledged the connection the two of them shared. Through whatever might come their way, Andrea's heart knew Devon was the one for her.

She hadn't come to Pine Creek searching for

anything but peace and a place to find herself. But what she found was worth so much more than that. She knew that God had guided her straight into Kate's life and all the way to Devon. She couldn't thank Him enough for knowing not only what she needed, but whom she needed, in her life.

CHAPTER THIRTY-TWO

Andrea slid into the bridesmaid dress and stared at her reflection in the mirror. She adored the light gray color with the added bling on her shoulder. Thankful for how everything had turned out, she accepted her final look and walked out of the dressing room staged at the main house.

Devon stood waiting nearby in the living room—a devilishly handsome look on his face—dressed to the nines with a tux and white, long-sleeved shirt that showed off his muscles in all the right places.

"You look stunningly gorgeous," Devon said, holding out his hand and twirling her around when she happily accepted it.

"I can say the same for you, cowboy," Andrea

stated matter-of-factly. "Gorgeous" might have been a loose term to describe the way Devon looked now, but she could easily find a few more to appease him. "You clean up nice."

"Well, look at that," Porter announced as he entered the living room. He was decked out in a tux, looking handsome as well. "You two look like a match made in heaven. Or however that saying goes."

Devon slapped a hand on his father's shoulder and let out a laugh. "Thanks, Pops."

"What do you say we round everyone up and head out there?" Porter glanced at the watch on his wrist and smiled. "It's nearing go time."

Andrea had spent the morning preparing Kate for the wedding, making sure the bride's hair was styled and her makeup was just right. She couldn't wait to see her best friend in the wedding dress, knowing without a doubt she was going to take everyone's breath away.

"I've got my camera," Mya called out above the commotion stirring in the house. "How about a few pictures?"

"How about we let you take pictures once we get to where we're going?"

Mya agreed with Porter as everyone followed him from the living room and out onto the porch. Diane hooked an arm through Porter's and smiled back at Andrea and Devon.

Following their lead, Devon held his arm out to Andrea before walking down the front porch steps. He led her to the hayrack attached to the best of their horses at the ranch. Mya snapped a few pictures as everyone climbed aboard and settled on the hay bales.

When Porter shot her a look, Mya shrugged and said a quick apology. "I can't help it. I need to capture every moment as it happens."

Andrea sat beside Devon as the horses led them to the barn. It was the perfect day for a wedding. The leaves on the trees were a lovely hue in autumn, and the weather was just right. September was gorgeous in North Dakota, and it showed off its seasonal colors so well that no one had to use their imagination to understand its beauty.

Even though Andrea had helped set up for the ceremony and reception, the sight of it still took her breath away. Hay bales covered with streams of silk lined the aisle, providing sensible seating for the guests. Rustic pails full of an autumn mixture lined the aisles, giving off fall vibes all the way around. Candles adorned the setting, providing a simple but stunning look as well.

Andrea hooked her arm around the crook of

Devon's elbow and walked toward the center aisle. Soft music played behind them in the barn, set to Kate and Beckett's playlist. Everything seemed like a stage in a romantic movie, coming together for a wedding day to remember.

Mya called out from behind them. They turned just in time to see the flash of her camera.

Andrea laughed but pleaded, "Please, take another one. We weren't ready."

"Okay, hurry up, we don't have all day," Mya said, ushering them together and playing the role of wedding photographer. Once Devon and Andrea were in place, Mya angled her camera and said, "Now look like you love each other."

"We do," Andrea said with a smile, ready for the camera's flash this time.

Apparently, Devon hadn't been ready—for the flash or for Andrea to say what she did. "We do?"

Andrea stared up at him, a smile pulling at her lips. It might have taken him by surprise, but she meant what she said. "I love you."

She reached up, resting a finger along his jawline. He tipped his head down, leaning in close to her and closing the distance between them. With a hand resting on her lower back, his nose touched hers just as the camera flashed.

"Perfect." Mya gave them a thumbs up, but clearly, neither of them were paying attention. Andrea was lost in her own moment with Devon, waiting for him to say those three magical words she wanted to hear.

"And I love you," he whispered, leaning in closer and pressing his lips against hers.

EPILOGUE

THREE MONTHS LATER

Snowflakes fell haphazardly outside while the family gathered around the living room at the main house.

The last three months were a blur as Andrea helped prepare the ranch for the winter months, not realizing how much time and energy it took.

Thankfully, it hadn't taken too much energy away from her, and she managed to spare some when it came to holding her precious goddaughter. When Kate told Andrea the news of declaring her the godmother of her bundle of joy, Andrea was beside herself with a love she'd never known before.

She sat beside Devon on the couch, cradling the small baby in her arms. Ava was everything Andrea imagined her to be, from her tiny fingers and toes to her little button nose. Her heart filled with love and adoration for baby Ava the moment she met her.

"How about you share her with the rest of us?" Porter asked, eager to hold his grandbaby. There was no doubt in Andrea's mind that this little girl was beyond blessed. The Carlson family would spoil her rotten, and have no regrets while doing so.

"We should probably get the Christmas decorations set up," Devon mentioned, nudging Andrea to hand Ava over to Porter.

She could sit there all day holding that little girl. Clearly, it wasn't ideal because things needed to be taken care of, but still.

With great protest, Andrea handed baby Ava to Porter. Her heart melted at the exchange between the grandfather and his grandchild. "You're so blessed, little Ava."

"I think you're wrong," Porter said, his face lighting up with pride. "We're the ones who are blessed."

Andrea couldn't disagree. Everything that happened at the ranch had been a blessing in disguise, but the baby was the cherry on top of it all.

"We'll be back," Andrea called out as Devon

guided her toward the door. She peeked around the corner once they were in the kitchen. "Just one more look."

"She'll still be here when we get back," Devon assured her. "I promise."

"I know," Andrea admitted sheepishly. "But it's just so sweet seeing Porter's eyes light up the way they are right now. And I don't want to miss these kinds of moments."

"There will be plenty of moments to share with Ava," Devon said, pulling Andrea away from the wall and leading her to the door. "But we need to help get things set up in time for Christmas. After last year, I guarantee the turnout around here will be off the charts."

Andrea heard wind about last year's Christmas events, and how William and Lacy had saved the tree farm from closing. It warmed her heart to know that this family pulled together when times were tough. She couldn't wait to see how this year's Christmas turned out at the ranch.

Decked out in winter gear, Andrea followed Devon from the house and walked beside him to the metal building. The building had done wonders for the reception, but now that it was over, Devon was right. They needed to finish getting it ready for Diane's lovely events.

"Is William going to dress up as Santa Claus again this year?" Andrea asked. She only asked because Lacy had filled her in about how they traveled into town on the sleigh the year before and how much the children loved it.

"I don't think so," Devon said with a shrug. "I don't think he cared too much for it."

"I thought Owen was the grinch, not Will—" Andrea cut herself off when she realized Owen was within earshot. She swallowed the lump in her throat, nervous that he might have overheard her.

Devon laughed and pulled her close to him. "It's okay. He already knows he's the Grinch of Pine Creek. Right, bro?"

Owen mumbled something under his breath and ventured into the metal building ahead of them. Andrea didn't know what to say, so she settled on saying, "I'm sorry. I didn't mean to say that."

Owen shrugged off her apology, seeming not to care too much. She still didn't know him well enough to judge whether he was truly a grinch, but he was grumpy—she would give him that.

"Oh, perfect," Diane called out from a nearby

booth. "I need your help with something really quick."

Owen turned back to Andrea and Devon, shooting them a look that said they were up before he dodged to the left and occupied himself with the mundane task of cleaning the small office.

"What do you need? I'll help," Andrea offered, making her way over to the booth decorated with wooden presents that weighed a ton. "As long as you don't have me move those, I'm all in."

Diane let out a light laugh and shook her head. "Oh, no, dear. Those are just fine where they are."

Andrea exchanged a look with Devon, confused as to what his mother needed her help with. Of course, Devon didn't provide much other than a shrug. Andrea supposed his guess was just as good as hers.

Without too much hesitation, Andrea approached the booth and readied herself for whatever task Diane needed her to complete. She was willing to do just about anything to help around the ranch, especially knowing this could be the best year yet for the activities and sales at the tree farm.

"First, I want you to know that you can say no if you truly aren't up for it," Diane started, giving

Andrea a concerned look. The look should have sent Andrea straight for the hills, but instead, she stood there, patiently waiting to hear her next mission. "There's this single mother who works at Sunrise Café. She's new in town. Just moved here at the end of November. From what I've heard, she just got out of a nasty marriage, and she doesn't have much."

There was no doubt in Andrea's mind whether she would get involved. The woman's story mirrored her own, except for the part of being a single mother. Andrea's heart was already invested.

"Say no more. I'm in," Andrea vowed.

Diane's eyes lit up like Andrea had promised to rope the moon. "You are? I haven't even mentioned what I wanted to tell you."

Andrea shrugged. "Do you have to? I mean, her story resonates with me, and knowing there's a child involved… Tell me what you need me to do."

Devon approached Andrea's side and grabbed her hand. Clearly, there was no way he heard what Diane said because he had been in the small office with Owen until now. But, then again, he had a sixth sense when it came to Andrea, so she figured he'd picked up something on the way over.

"Noel's such a sweetheart," Diane continued,

decorating the booth while she talked. "She can't be more than three or four years old."

Andrea's heart skipped in her chest. She didn't know where Diane was going with this, but if that little girl needed someone to step in and take care of her, Andrea would in a heartbeat. No questions asked.

"Do they need a place to stay?" Andrea's voice nearly squeaked. "We can find a place for them to stay. I know Devon and I aren't officially married, and living together might be frowned upon, but I'm willing to move in with him and give them my cabin."

Diane reached out and patted Andrea's arm. It did nothing to settle the thoughts running through her mind. She couldn't fathom being all alone in a town she didn't know without anywhere to go. Especially after a nasty divorce.

"All is well where that's concerned," Diane said with a soft smile. "No worries there. If that had been the case, I would've already loaded them up and brought them here."

Andrea exchanged a look with Devon. Owen was now standing by Devon's side, wondering what all the commotion was about.

"I'm just afraid that she won't be able to give that little girl a Christmas to remember, is all," Diane admitted, the soft smile fading into a frown. "It breaks my heart to know that Savannah's doing everything she can, but it might not be enough."

Owen coughed, and everyone turned to look at him. Andrea raised a brow, concerned with whether he was okay. He lifted a hand. "I'm good."

It was Devon's turn to ask the questions. "What do you need us to do? I'm sure we can figure something out."

"Well, I was hoping that someone would invite her to the ranch for the holidays," Diane said, her lips pulling into a kind smile. "At least then I'd know the little girl would enjoy Christmas, and her mother would, too."

Andrea looked from Devon to Owen. Owen looked as uncomfortable with the idea as she imagined he would be. At least knowing how grumpy the man was, Andrea didn't expect him to jump at the opportunity.

"I'll do it."

Andrea nearly lost her footing, and if it hadn't been for Devon holding her hand, she might have fallen over. Judging by the look on both Diane's and Devon's faces, she wasn't the only one surprised by Owen's offer to be the one to invite Savannah and Noel to the ranch during the upcoming festivities.

She didn't know what else to do other than pray

he truly wasn't the Grinch of Pine Creek, and that he would be able to help give the little girl and her mother a Christmas to remember.

Don't miss Owen & Savannah's story! Grab it today!
A Pine Creek Holiday

ABOUT THE AUTHOR

Christina Butrum launched her writing career in 2015 with the release of The Fairshore Series.

Writing contemporary fiction, she brings realistic situations with swoon-worthy romance to the pages - allowing her readers to fall in love right along with the characters.

When she isn't busy writing, Christina enjoys spending time with her family. Christina Butrum looks forward to publishing many more books for her readers to enjoy.

www.authorchristinabutrum.myshopify.com

Sign Up for Christina's Newsletter Here:
https://www.subscribepage.com/authorcbutrum
Join Christina's Group Here:
https://www.facebook.com/groups/
ButrumsBookBabes

- facebook.com/authorcbutrum
- twitter.com/authorcbutrum
- amazon.com/author/christinabutrum
- bookbub.com/profile/christina-butrum

SALES, BUNDLES AND MORE

Hi there!

Thank you so much for reading my book! Whether it's your 1st or 34th, I'm glad you're here. I appreciate you!

Check out my Shopify store @ authorchristinabutrum.myshopify.com for latest releases, sales, bundles, and more!

Made in United States
North Haven, CT
22 November 2024